House
on
March Lane

Michelle Briscombe

The right of Michelle Briscombe to be identified as the
Author of the Work has been asserted by her in accordance
with the Copyright, Designs and Patents Act 1988.

Copyright © Michelle Briscombe 2016

THE HOUSE ON MARCH LANE

FIRST EDITION
- 2016 -

Published by
Candy Jar Books
Mackintosh House
136 Newport Road, Cardiff, CF24 1DJ
www.candyjarbooks.co.uk

A catalogue record of this book is available
from the British Library

ISBN: 978-0-9933221-2-9

Cover illustration
Copyright © Hannah Peck

Printed and bound in the UK by
CPI Group (UK) Ltd, Croydon, CR0 4YY

In loving memory of Therese,
my mother-in-law and friend.
And in celebration of everything that she
brought to our lives.

CHAPTER ONE

Harriet sat at her dressing table, staring out of the window. She could hardly contain her excitement and certainly couldn't concentrate on writing in her diary. Papa was returning home today and that very thought turned the butterflies in her stomach into giant, swooping birds. He had been away for far too long and although he had sent parcels and had written often, his letters came irregularly, sometimes none for a whole month and then three or four in the same week.

She had missed him so much; five years was too long. In that time she had grown from a small child of eight into a young lady of thirteen. He would hardly recognise her! But the letters had kept them in touch and the parcels, with their exotic contents, were a wonder to her. The thrill and excitement of his return was mirrored by the expectation of what he would bring back with him.

She stood and began to pace the room. The light from the windows was filtered by the heavy brocade curtains. Her mama said that sunlight was bad for her skin and that she was to keep the curtains partly drawn, and always carry a parasol when outside. But sometimes, when she knew her mama was not at home, Harriet would throw open the windows and lean out as far as she dared just to feel the warmth of the sun on her face. And other times she would skip into the garden and sit under the willow tree, its leafy fingers touching the ground like a delicate cage, and she would remove her tight buttoned boots and stockings and enjoy the tickle of the cool grass between her toes.

She had an adventurous spirit and knew that it was inherited from her papa, though she would never be able to follow in his footsteps. If only she had been born a boy! Her grandmother, who thought Harriet to be spoilt and quite un-ladylike was always warning that she *should be seen and not heard.*

There was a knock on her bedroom door.

'Enter,' said Harriet in the grown-up way that she had been practicing for her papa.

Lily came into the room, 'Miss, your mama has sent me to collect you. She says you are to get changed at once because a carriage has been called for Joseph to accompany you both to the station, where you are to wait until the master's train arrives.'

Harriet's attempt at being mature quickly vanished.

'Oh, Lily! Can you help me choose something to wear please? And we must be quick! I want to look my best for Papa!' she cried, her excitement overwhelming her again.

'What about the damson dress with the beads?' Lily asked, hurrying to the enormous oak wardrobe that brooded in the alcove like a giant waiting to pounce.

'Yes, that's a lovely dress, thank you.'

Lily pulled at the doors and separated the many garments until she found the one she was searching for. She removed it delicately from its silk hanger and passed it to Harriet who was already in her petticoat; her pinafore in a heap on the rug at her feet.

Lily helped her quickly.

'How do I look?' Harriet asked.

'Beautiful! Your papa will hardly recognise you,' Lily smiled warmly.

Harriet hugged Lily and then rushed towards the door, turning briefly she said, 'Thank you, Lily, you are such a good friend!' and then she was gone.

Lily went to collect the discarded clothes. She really did like Harriet, she had a good heart. They were the same age and whilst their worlds were miles apart, almost as far as the master had travelled, they were indeed good friends and had been since she had started work at the house almost two years ago.

She hoped that it wouldn't change when the master returned.

CHAPTER TWO

Flora looked up at the huge sign that glared at her in the bright autumn sunlight. Gold lettering on a burgundy background: *Theodore and Daughter.*

She sighed. Her dad had been promising to put up the sign since she was six. She was thirteen now and had been hoping for most of those years that this day would never come. As much as she loved her dad the last thing she'd ever wanted to do was work in the family business.

Her dad had inherited the business from her grandfather, who had inherited it from his father, an age-old tradition between father and son. As Flora was his only child, her dad was ensuring that one day it would be hers.

But Flora had other ideas. She was going to be a police detective, a crime solver with an exciting life filled with mysterious cases and clues – a female Sherlock Holmes! She wasn't sure why her dad thought she would want the family business because as long as she could remember she'd been telling anyone who would listen that a detective was what she intended to be.

She strolled into the yard.

Colin was sat in his oversized kennel; his ferocious grin greeted her together with a wave of his tail. She was the only person who ever got a welcome from him. A big

German shepherd, he was every bit as fierce as his breed expected him to be. He was, after all, the guardian of all her dad's treasures. Flora went to him and knelt down. She was rewarded with an abundance of licks from his rough tongue, his tail telling her how happy he was to see her.

Flora and Colin had a relationship that no one could believe; he was the master of this yard and only she received his affections. Even Flora's dad kept him at a distance, although Colin was respectful to him because he provided his daily meals.

'Hello, boy,' Flora smiled, 'have you missed me?' Colin continued to lick and wag.

'You know what's in there, go on dig in,' Colin poked his long, dark snout deep into the pocket of her silver coat and quickly found the treat. 'See you later, we'll go for a nice walk,' she said as she stood up. 'Don't go biting anyone today okay?' Colin turned his head to the side as if he was deciding whether or not to take her advice.

Flora made her way into the large warehouse that stood in the middle of the yard. The smell always washed over her the moment she stepped inside: Wood. Old wood. Creosote. Bitumen – a thousand different smells that told so many different stories.

Her father owned a reclamation and salvage yard.

Hundreds of years' worth of objects were encased both inside the warehouse building and outside in the yard. Paraphernalia of every possible type: wood, metal, brick, marble, clay and terracotta – stripped from old houses, crumbling stately homes, run down pubs, Edwardian schools, Victorian hospitals and soon-to-be renovated restaurants – all had a place in her father's warehouse. Some of the items and even some furniture, had been there since her great-grandfather had started the business almost a hundred years before.

When people were restoring old houses or buildings and they needed something authentic they came to her dad to buy and to sell. If they wanted antique wood block flooring, it was upstairs in a room piled to the ceiling. If they wanted a church pew, there were fifty of them in an area at the back, leant reverently against the walls. Doors of every size and shape stripped back to their original oak, poplar or pine were housed in units that her father had made.

Rough floorboards and heavy oak beams, floor tiles, fire tiles, flagstones, cobblestones and staddle stones. Cast iron and marble fireplaces, clay chimney pots, slate roof tiles, wrought iron railings and gates, time-worn roll-top baths on legs and cracked Belfast sinks, brass handles, door knobs, hinges and locks. All stacked neatly in its rightful place, both inside and out.

You name it, her dad usually sold it. However, absolutely nothing inside his warehouse or outside in the yard was new. No modern plastic windows – no way! He sold only items from another time, a time before electric lighting and definitely before PVC windows and doors. The warehouse made the most interesting and fantastic playground that Flora had ever played in but she still didn't want it to be hers.

'Oh, there you are, lovely,' her father greeted her with his usual bear hug. Wrapped in his arms Flora could smell the wood varnish that was his familiar aftershave.

'Dad!' she cried, her voice muffled by his old jumper. 'I only saw you at breakfast!'

'Sorry,' he said finally releasing her. 'Wondered if I'd see you today. What did you think?' He waited for Flora to respond then prompted '...of the sign!? Do you like it?'

Flora forced a smile, 'Yes, yes it's... um... lovely.'

Her father seemed disappointed at her reply and she didn't want to hurt his feelings. 'I mean it's great. I love the colours too. Thanks, Dad.' She put on her best fake smile and he seemed to believe her.

'I'm glad you like them. I thought that burgundy and gold, well that they were appropriate for a girl.' He beamed and Flora felt terrible for lying to him. She quickly changed the subject.

'Is it alright if Archie comes over? We could carry on sorting out the tile room.'

Archie was her best friend and they had been inseparable since reception class.

'Yes that's fine. I've got some bookwork to do, so you can help if we have a rush of customers.'

Her dad had a little office tucked away at the back of the warehouse. His computer was the only modern item that was allowed in his yard but even that was ancient and dated in Flora's opinion.

Colin's low growl alerted them to someone outside and Flora turned to see a young couple walk in.

Her father was distracted as he called out, 'Hello, come in, come in! Don't mind Colin out there, just doing his job but he's soft as a brush really.'

Flora raised her eyebrows as she heard her dad doing what he liked to do best – talk.

She climbed the two sets of creaky wooden stairs to the third floor and walked past the stained glass windows arranged neatly against the wall.

Her dad had made several rooms in the spacious upstairs space of the old warehouse, using partition walls he had created six rooms on the second floor and another two on the third. Each was filled with all manner of things. Only three of them had natural light; the room she was heading for had a large skylight and housed the huge collection of tiles. The tiles were placed in precarious piles and in deep wooden chests and Flora wanted to spend some time sorting them into age, colours and styles. She liked to do small jobs for her dad because despite her reluctance to own the business, she had inherited his trait of being organised and tidy. She also liked to hone her detective skills and work out which tiles matched or belonged together.

As she walked into the room a breath of air touched her face as if someone had gently brushed her cheek with a feather. Flora was startled and looked up at the skylight. It was closed. She spun around quickly. *What on earth was that?* For a moment she hesitated.

Silly girl, you've been playing here since you were two! She quickly dismissed her unease with a small smile.

The autumn sun shone in a powder blue sky above her as she sat down on the dusty rug in the middle of the room. She was soon distracted by the designs of the tiles as she dug into a box.

CHAPTER THREE

Flora was startled when Archie charged in at breakneck speed. She hadn't even heard him climb the stairs.

'Oh! You made me jump!' she cried as he flung himself down onto the rug next to her.

'Sorry,' he grinned.

Archie was his usual dishevelled self. His faded yellow sweatshirt was torn at the shoulder seam, a pair of old tatty jeans had a rip in one knee and his trainers were caked in dried mud. His curly hair matched the colour of his sweatshirt perfectly and was standing up as though he had just stuck his finger in an electric socket. All in all Archie was a mess, which was exactly why he was so special to her.

'Have you finished?' he asked, his dark grey eyes smiling as he glanced at the stacks of tiles that surrounded her like a small fortress.

'Not yet, I've got loads more boxes to do.'

'I've brought some sarnies, we could have dinner then I can help,' Archie said throwing off his rucksack and diving in. That was another thing she loved about Archie, his prepared and supersonic approach to everything. She was already imagining what the sandwiches would look like as he pulled out a large plastic tub and opened the lid.

The smell of salami wafted to her. The white bread held at least six slices of salami in each – a feast!

'I'll go and wash my hands, they're filthy from the tiles,' she said getting up. 'Be back in a sec,' and she quickly left the room.

Archie looked around. He liked spending time with Flora. She was his best friend but more importantly, he knew just how much they both needed each other.

Flora's mum had left when she was just a year old, leaving Flora and her dad behind like they were litter dropped in the street. They hadn't seen her since that day. Flora was happy living with her dad and couldn't even remember her mother but Archie knew she often wondered how her mum could have done such a terrible thing.

Not having your mum around was something that Archie understood too well. His mother was more concerned with her own life and barely cared for him at all. She provided the house, paid the bills and bought the food; everything else was up to him. Since he could remember he had taken care of himself. He got up alone in the mornings and made his own breakfast. He'd learned how to cook his tea in the evenings, do his homework without help and go to bed each night without so much as a 'goodnight.' Sometimes days would go by and he wouldn't see his mother, or he might pass her briefly as she came in to the house when he was going out. As he got older she left money for him to buy clothes or shoes. She worked shifts in a factory and he felt as though he hardly knew her. It was as if he was her son only by birth. He thought that there must have been a time when he was a very small, that she had taken care of him, though it was a memory that would not come. He'd never known his dad and so he understood some of what Flora felt about her mum.

Archie knew that his was not a normal life and that his mother didn't behave like a proper parent should, which was why he took any opportunity he could to get away from it, being with Flora every day helped. School, learning and exams were his main priority too. He wasn't stupid and he knew that he needed an education if he was ever to escape his life at home.

Flora came back into the room, 'OK, Jamie Oliver, what have you cooked for us today?' she said warmly and together they tucked into the sandwiches, crisps and Coke that Archie had brought.

Saturday night was fish and chip night. Flora, Archie and her dad were sat in front of the wood burner with their tea on their laps. The room was cosy and warm. Archie always stayed for chippy supper on a Saturday. Her dad bought it on the way home from the yard, their Saturday treat. The strong smell of vinegar filled the air.

'How did you get on with those tiles?' her dad asked, wiping his fingers on a tea-towel.

'Good,' said Flora.

'We've nearly finished the big crate,' Archie said between chips.

'You can come tomorrow, if you like,' said her dad.

Flora was surprised, he didn't usually open the yard on

a Sunday, he often told her that Sunday was a day of rest. They always took Colin for a walk then went for a drive in the van, sometimes they would poke around in the odd skip for antiquities that people had no idea about. Flora loved to see the look on their faces when her dad offered to buy something that they'd thrown into the big yellow waste bins.

'Why, Dad? You never work on Sunday,' Flora asked.

'Only this once, love, I've got to finish that bookwork. I'm not opening up. I just need to use the computer,' he smiled at her.

'You can use my laptop. I don't have any homework.'

'No, no. I only understand the software on the computer at the warehouse. It'll only take an hour or two, then we can go for a nice stroll and have some lunch. Do you fancy coming?'

Flora smiled, 'Yes I'll come. Archie?'

Archie's mouth was still full of chips and he nodded with a smile.

'Great, we'll leave about ten, get sorted and be out of there by midday.' Her dad wiped his chin and then screwed up his chip paper before leaning over and throwing it into the wood burner.

CHAPTER FOUR

Harriet loved to go to the city. She went occasionally with her mama to collect her grandmother when she came to stay. The bustling busyness both inside and outside the railway station always thrilled her. As the driver pulled the carriage to the kerb and Joseph jumped down, she watched the black Hansom cabs outside jostling to get the best position to collect passengers. The horses were whinnying at each other and their drivers calling out for fares. The noise at the station was like a great lion's roar: street vendors shouting, hooves on cobblestones and creaking wheels on carriages. The roads were crowded with more people than Harriet had ever seen – hundreds of people and all of them trying to speak at once! The city was both intoxicating and frightening at the same time.

Inside the carriage her mama gave her instructions. 'You must hold my hand at all times, Harriet. I do not want you to get lost. I am quite sure we would never find you amongst these hoards.'

Her mama turned up her nose with distaste; she hated to come to the city almost as much as Harriet loved it. In fact, Harriet often thought that she and her mother could not be more different. It made her sad sometimes; she would have liked to have been closer to her, especially since

Papa had been away. But she did understand that her mama missed her father and sometimes would seem distant and lonely and Harriet was not too young to feel it. At least in that respect, they both felt the same.

She held tightly on to her mother's hand as they walked into the cavernous station. It smelled of dusty coal and smoke. The whistles and whoosh of the steam trains made Harriet jump with delight. She saw an old man playing an accordion, a cap at his feet and a monkey, of all things, on his shoulder! Harriet wanted to break free from her mother's grip and run over to him, drop a sixpence in his cap and touch the monkey's golden fur but she knew better than to disobey her mama. People rushed past her carrying leather bags and cases, pulling tin trunks and chattering to one another. Harriet imagined the exotic journeys they might be going on to far-away places, just like her papa.

'Your papa's train is due at twenty-five past twelve. This is the correct platform, so we shall wait.' Her mama squeezed her hand and Harriet smiled at her, for now both of them were joined by the same feeling of anticipation.

Harriet stared at the huge station clock as it slowly counted down the minutes until she would see her father again.

As though it was breathing in deeply and expelling its last cloudy breath, the great train pulled into the station. Her mama pulled Harriet back from the edge as the steam hissed and pushed out great white billows along the platform. The roar echoed inside Harriet's head; her ears felt like they did when she was under the water in the bath tub and she giggled. The magnificent engine announced its final stop with a deafening screech of the brakes.

Crowds of people emptied from the train, barging and pushing past them in a terrible hurry to be somewhere else now that their journey had come to an end. Harriet's heart was beating so hard she could hear it.

Searching anxiously for her papa's face she stood on her tip toes so that she could look along the line of brown and cream carriages. When almost all of the people had gone, through the last wisps of steam, she finally saw her beloved papa.

He was dressed in his uniform; his white cotton breeches were tucked into his long leather boots and although he was not wearing his officer's hat, he still wore his navy coat. The buttons were shining as was the gold trim on his cuffs and the tails of the dark coat fell smartly behind him. He was still every bit the handsome officer and sailor that Harriet remembered.

Harriet and her mama began to walk towards him, she was trying so hard to contain herself, to behave as a lady would but when her papa opened his arms she tugged free from her mother's tight fingers, lifted her skirt and ran as she often did in the garden when no one was watching. She flew into his arms and he caught her and turned her around and around like she was seven years old again.

'Harriet, how you have grown!' her papa said loudly into her hair. He put her down and held her out to look at her. 'Just as beautiful as your mama!' he cried and pulled her to him again.

Then she was caught in an embrace between her mama and papa, squashed in the middle and not caring one bit if people were scandalised. When they finally separated it felt to Harriet as though the barrier of their time had descended again. Her mama stepped back a little, as though she had shocked herself at the way she had behaved in such a public place.

'How nice it is to see you, William,' her mama said and held out her hand. Harriet felt ashamed that that was all her mama could find to say.

'And you too, Charlotte.' He took her hand formally, yet there was a twinkle in his eye and a smile on his face. Harriet was relieved, Papa that had left five years ago was still the same person; he had not changed.

'Shall we go home ladies? Joseph will bring my cases and trunks. There is so much I have to tell you.'

Harriet, and then her mama, took one arm each and together the three of them walked from the station out into the noisy street, to their carriage and home.

CHAPTER FIVE

'Do you think this one matches those other green ones?' Archie asked passing a pretty but slightly cracked tile to Flora.

'Um, yes I think it does,' Flora said taking it from him and examining it closely.

They'd been sitting on the rug sorting tiles into age, colours and styles for a few hours.

The sky had changed from yesterday's blue to a mean charcoal grey that threw hard and brittle rain at the glass above them. Flora was glad they were inside and not out walking Colin. The room was heated by a bulky antique radiator which had been removed from a Victorian hospital; it kept them warm but they were still wrapped in jumpers, hats and fingerless gloves. The warehouse was, after all, a hundred years old and prone to drafts that could feel like mini tornados when the wind was blowing in the right direction.

Archie picked up another tile and wiped it with a cloth revealing a deep red tile edged with tiny blue and white flowers. He took out another and wiped again. It matched. He delved deeper into the old box, pulling out tile after sooty tile until Flora realised what he was doing.

'Oh, I think it's a floor,' she said standing up. 'Look, the flowers connect together.' She joined him and they cleaned and placed the tiles down on the old warehouse boards.

When they were finished they'd arranged a hundred and seventy-seven tiles and it was quite spectacular. In the middle of the floor was a Celtic circle with a small, white rose at its centre but the very last tile, the heart of the rose, was missing; the final piece of the beautiful jigsaw.

'My dad will love this. I think it's Georgian; probably dates from around the 1820s. It's really unusual to find a whole floor and in such good condition. I wonder where it came from.'

'There's a sticker on the crate,' said Archie peering at a faded yellow label. 'It says March Lane but there's no house number or town.'

'I'll ask my dad, I'm sure he'll have something written in his catalogues,' Flora said. 'It's a shame about the last tile though. Let's have a look, see if we can find it.'

They both searched in the numerous crates for the last piece of the puzzle. Flora was enthralled; she loved to put together little pieces of history so that someone else might enjoy them again.

They rummaged through the dusty boxes, pulling out more and more tiles, until the room was untidier than when they'd begun.

'Oh dear, no tile and look at the state of the room!' Flora exclaimed seeing the mess they'd made.

'It's okay, we can tidy up after school and at the weekend,' Archie smiled, he knew how important order was to Flora.

'I know... but wouldn't it have been great to find it?'

'Don't worry. I bet we'll come across it. Do you want to leave this down for now?' he asked, looking at the striking floor that they'd unearthed.

'Yes. I'll show Dad tomorrow. Let's go and find him, I'm sure it's nearly lunch time.'

Archie led the way from the room but stopped so suddenly that Flora bumped into him.

'Did you feel that?' Archie turned around quickly, his face had grown pale.

'What? Archie?' she asked.

'Something touched my cheek. It felt like, like a....'

'...Feather,' Flora finished. 'I felt it yesterday when I was up here. I think it was just a draft...' though she already knew that she didn't sound very convincing.

'It wasn't a draft. It was real... Something... touched my face.' Archie's hand was shaking as he held it to his cheek.

Flora had never seen him look so upset. She led him back into the room and made him sit down on the rug, though she could tell he was reluctant to do so.

'Archie, it's always draughty in here. Remember that time in the yard when the leaves started to fly around in the wind and came through the door and across the warehouse floor?' She smiled, trying to reassure him but she was feeling quite unsettled by his reaction. Archie was always brave, he had too much going on in his troubled life to be afraid of anything.

'It wasn't the wind,' Archie said harshly and then he

spoke so quietly that Flora had to crouch down to hear him, '… something… whispered my name.'

CHAPTER SIX

'What do you mean, *something* whispered your name?' Flora asked.

'It didn't sound like a person, it didn't sound human. But... it said my name. I can't explain. It touched my face and then it said *Archie* like it was inside my head,' Archie swallowed hard, he was trying not to cry. He was terrified and was certain, beyond doubt, that it had been a ghost. If Flora didn't believe him he wouldn't know what he would do. He gave her a half-hearted smile, '...think I've just been haunted,' he said quietly.

Flora knew that whatever had happened had been real. Archie didn't live in a fantasy world; his life was harsh and sometimes cruel and he would never allow his imagination to take over. It would be too awful to return to reality.

Flora's dad had threatened to ring social services about Archie's mum but Flora had begged him not to. Even if they'd offered Archie a place to live with them, her dad was a single parent and the social services might not agree. Archie would probably end up in foster care and then there was always the possibility that Flora would never see him again.

She had told her dad that Archie's mother didn't starve him or hurt him, she was just indifferent, though she knew that that was just as bad. Her dad had agreed not to report her and they'd made a pact: they would take care of Archie, forever if they had to. Flora and her dad would be his family. As long as Archie had them, he would always be alright.

'I believe you,' she whispered. 'I felt it earlier but sort of pretended to myself that it was just a draft, only... nothing spoke to me.' She saw the relief on Archie's face and was glad she'd been honest.

'What do you think it wanted?' she dared to ask, looking around at the creeping darkness of the room.

'I don't know and I don't want to stay and find out. Shall we go and – '

'Ah! There you are! I've been calling you. Didn't you hear me?' Flora's dad bounded into the room and they both jumped. Flora looked at Archie, and they started to giggle manically.

'Good grief, you both look like you've seen a ghost! Now come on, I've finished what I needed to do, let's go and walk Colin then get some Sunday lunch.' Without waiting for them or even noticing the tile floor and the surrounding mess, he turned and left as quickly as he'd come in.

After their walk they stopped at a carvery for lunch and over their food Flora told her dad about the floor that they'd uncovered. She didn't mention anything about Archie's experience and was glad to see that the colour had returned to his cheeks, especially once a lamb dinner, roast vegetables and gravy was put in front of him. Her dad was very interested.

'What did it say on the label?' he asked.

'March Lane,' Flora said looking at Archie for confirmation.

Archie nodded.

'March Lane doesn't ring any bells. Perhaps it's an old crate. Where did you find it?'

'I pulled it out from a corner last week.'

'Mmm… a bit of a mystery. It'll be in the catalogues. Perhaps you've unearthed something that was there from before my time. There are plenty of those in the old girl.'

'Old girl' was a term her dad used when he talked about the warehouse.

He took a sip of water. 'It took me three weeks to move some of that furniture around when I built the rooms upstairs. Most of it has been there since before I was born. Perhaps now would be a good time to have a sort out. Get rid of a few things that haven't sold. Old Mr Wessel will be happy to take a few pieces away.'

Mr Wessel had an antique shop on the high street. He bought and sold second-hand furniture and he often came to the warehouse poking around for a bargain. Flora didn't like him. He was sly. His black eyes were always darting around and he looked so much like a weasel, with sharp pointy features and eyes that were too close together, that she'd had to stop herself from calling him Mr *Weasel* whenever she saw him. It always felt like he was trying to get one over on her dad, who was good and kind to everyone.

'I'll give him a call. So what was all the shrieking and giggling about earlier?' her dad asked.

'Oh n... n... nothing...' Flora stammered.

'We were just concentrating on the tiles, you startled us, that's all,' Archie said jumping to Flora's rescue.

Fortunately her dad had already picked up the menu and wasn't listening to his answer, 'Right then, who wants "death by chocolate"?' he asked.

When they got home her dad put the kettle on whilst Flora went upstairs to put on her onesie. It was only six o'clock but it was dark outside and she wanted to curl up for the rest of the evening in front of the wood burner. They'd dropped Archie home because he had homework to do and Flora had felt sorry for him going into a dark, empty house.

The rain was still battering the window and although the heating was on full she shivered. She sat on her bed and thought about Archie and what he'd heard in the warehouse.

Flora had never been frightened there. When things weren't going well in school or if she started thinking about her mother too much, the warehouse was the one place she would want to be, now she wasn't sure how she felt.

Flora didn't believe in ghosts. If she was going to be an important detective one day she wouldn't be able to use ghostly sightings as a way to solve crimes, she would need real clues and hard evidence. She'd once read that the police used psychics to find missing people sometimes, although she didn't really believe it. But she did believe Archie and if he said *something* had whispered his name then Flora believed *something* had.

Her dad called her and she knew a mug of tea and chocolate fingers would be waiting. She put on her slippers and went down to their cosy little room where the fire was burning and welcoming her.

CHAPTER SEVEN

The old building sighed softly in the stormy night. It wrapped its arms around all inside like the embrace of a mother holding onto her children. In quiet corners mice stirred and scurried.

Outside in his kennel the dog watched silently, wagging his tail in greeting as visitors, old and new brushed past him without a sound in the darkness.

In a room, high in the attic, a figure moved, so transparent that you might only notice it from the corner of your eye but if you turned to look it would be gone in a shimmer of air. The transparent person, for that was what she once had been, was so melancholy, so desperately sad that even the old building could do nothing to calm her.

As she swirled from one space to another her hopeless need for help became so intense that her very existence in a world where she did not belong caused things around her to move. The stacks of tiles left behind by the two children toppled over and crashed loudly in the stillness. The floor on which she had once stood as a living person began to spin, high and wide into the air, dancing a sorry jig without music, then cracking and braking as it fell into a jumbled jigsaw to the floor.

In a single breath she was outside, gazing down at the dog in its kennel. The dog's tail wagged again, he was used to the strange and lonely figures that took shelter in his domain. These wisps of *people never caused him harm and he knew he did not need to defend either himself or his master's property from them. They lived together in understanding harmony. Yet he felt this one's pain so strongly that his tail stopped moving and his ears fell flat against his head as he released a pitiful whimper. He knew every detail of her sorrow but could do nothing to help her. Then she was gone and he rested his head on his enormous paws, still holding onto her sadness like a present she had given him.*

Inside the warehouse the girl, for that was what she had once been, stopped in the tile room. She waited, calmer, quieter, now knowing what she had to do.

CHAPTER EIGHT

The chatter of voices in the hallway above alerted Lily that the family had returned. It was her job to collect hats and coats and put them away in the hallway cupboard. She raced up the stairs from the kitchen, as fast as she could. Her hands trembled at the thought of meeting the master. Even though the mistress could be formidable, Lily still felt an underlying kindness from her that she could not put her finger on but which she knew was there somewhere.

She'd heard some terrible things about masters from her four sisters, all of who were in service. They could be cruel and dismissive, or sometimes just plain nasty. Her sister, Mary, worked for a mine owner in the north and was only allowed a half Sunday off every two months. This meant that Lily rarely saw her but the brief notes she received were always filled with tales of how mean the master had been to both people and animals alike. Lily thought often about those terrible stories and said a prayer each night since she had heard the master was returning, she hoped that he would not turn out to be the same.

Mr Wickes had already answered the door and welcomed the master home and was now coming back down the stairs. He was the butler and wasn't a bad lot. He took his duties very seriously but was a fair person to work for. He wasn't overly friendly but Lily knew his intentions were always good.

'No need to run, Lily. Now straighten your collar before you go up,' he said as he passed her on the stairs. She stopped for a moment to compose herself before she entered the hallway. She waited for the family to notice her and give her their outdoor clothes. The floor tiles that she'd polished early that morning were almost sparkling. She was so glad she'd given them an extra buff. The prettiness of the blue and white pattern always cheered her up, even though she felt like she cleaned it most of her life.

Noticing Lily for the first time Harriet caught the sleeve of her uniform and pulled her towards her papa. Lily was horrified.

'Papa, this is Lily, whom I spoke to you about.'

The master stood frighteningly tall above her and then to Lily's absolute relief he smiled gently, 'Ah, Lily. Yes Harriet has told me much about you in her many letters whilst I was away. She said you have become friends.'

Lily was so shocked by his kind words that she forgot to curtsy and could do nothing but nod her head stupidly.

'Well I wouldn't exactly say friends,' Harriet's mother said quickly, but then she smiled too, 'but she has become a very good housemaid, she has learned quickly. She also knows how to read and write, isn't that correct Lily?'

Lily was astonished and continued to nod foolishly. Could it be that her prayers had been answered? Not only did the master seem nice and kind, but in the time that the mistress had been outside the door she too had softened and come back a different person! Lily gathered herself and finally remembered what she was supposed to be doing, she managed a small curtsey, 'It's very nice to meet you, sir. May I take your coat?'

'Yes, thank you... and a belated welcome to our home. I hope you will be happy here.'

Then to Lily's amazement he turned to Harriet and her mother and put his arms around them. They both leaned into him and then walked into the parlour, all three forgetting to give her their outdoor clothing. Lily decided not to chase after them and left them to it. They would call when they needed her.

She went back downstairs to the kitchen wearing a huge smile. Cook was making the dinner for the master's return and was rushing around the kitchen. Cook was a tall, thin woman whose size and stature belied her occupation. Her grey, wiry hair was held back in a tight bun and Lily thought she looked more like a stern school mistress than a maker of extraordinarily tasty pies.

'What's that big smile about? You look like the cat that got the cream,' Cook said harshly. She was always in a terrible mood at dinner time. She was a perfectionist and woe-betide anyone who upset Cook when she was making a treacle sponge pudding!

'I just met the master and he's lovely!' said Lily, still smiling.

'Well I told you not to worry, didn't I?' Cook said a

little more gently, 'He's a good 'un the master, best one I ever worked for. Terrible shame he's been away so long. Never thought he'd be gone for five years! He only signed up for two but that Mr Darwin had other ideas. Be interesting to see what comes out of that journey all around the world. Papers say Mr Darwin's made some discoveries. Well I hope he don't take the master on any more blinkin' journey's, don't think the mistress or young Harriet could take 'im goin' away again. Now hand me that dish and take that stupid look off your face, bet you can't believe your luck, girl.'

And she was right; Lily *could not* believe her luck.

CHAPTER NINE

Flora and Archie decided to go back to the warehouse in daylight the following Saturday. It was too dark in the evenings after school now that the autumn nights were drawing into winter, and they just weren't brave enough to go to the tile room with night pressing at the window.

Archie was still convinced that something had said his name and Flora still believed him. Now all they had to do was go back to the scene of the crime and see if they could work out *why* it had happened. Quickly manoeuvring past Flora's dad, who was chatting to customers in the outside yard, they tentatively climbed the stairs.

The corridor leading to the tile room seemed gloomier to Flora, like someone had changed the light bulb to the lowest possible wattage. There was a stillness too that she couldn't quite understand, a stillness that was never normally there. The warehouse made lots of noises; creaking pipes, squeaky floorboards, dripping water, whistling wind, there was always some sound – but not today. The furthest corners of the long corridor seemed cloaked in a murkiness that Flora had never noticed.

'Does it seem darker up here than normal?' Archie asked, as if reading her mind.

'I was just thinking that exact same thing,' Flora said,

feeling anxious.

'This is spooky,' Archie laughed nervously.

They walked through the door and both of them stopped.

Flora gasped.

The tiles that they'd left in piles around the room had all been pushed over. Some of them were broken and cracked where they'd fallen. The room was in disarray. It seemed as though the tiles has been stood like dominoes and then kicked over, one knocking into the next. But worst of all was the Georgian floor. The beautiful red and blue tiles were smashed into a million tiny fragments. Flora took a frightened step backwards through the doorway but Archie stayed where he was.

'Well if there was any doubt...' he whispered hoarsely.

'You don't think someone broke in last night...' but even as she spoke, Flora knew she didn't believe it. There were lots of expensive antiques in the warehouse, that's why they kept Colin as a guard dog. Who would break in and walk up two flights of stairs just to destroy some old floor tiles?

Flora took a deep breath.

'Come on, let's have a closer look,' she finally suggested, bravely moving around Archie and walking into the room.

Archie followed slowly and she could hear him breathing heavily like he'd just run a race. She could sense his fear but instead of making her more scared, it gave her courage.

'Well, whatever it is, it wanted to let us know something and it *must* be about the floor.'

Archie was staring at the broken pieces. He was terrified and Flora knew that she had to distract him.

'Let's treat this as a crime scene. What would Sherlock Holmes do?' she said quickly.

'He would look for clues,' Archie replied softly.

'And who would he ask?'

'He would ask Dr Watson for some ideas but really he'd know the answers all along,' Archie said. He understood what Flora was trying to do and he was grateful.

'Alright, Dr Archie, what do you see in front of you?' Flora said briskly.

'A big mess and a scarily ruined floor.'

'Anything else?'

Archie shook his head.

'What about the shape of the tiles?' All Archie could see was a mound of tiny coloured shards. He shook his head again and shivered. He was scared that if he spoke too loudly the "whatever it was" would whisper in his ear again.

'Look closer,' said Flora. Despite her nervousness she was starting to enjoy herself.

And then Archie saw it – the little blue and white flowers had been separated and placed on top of all the red pieces creating a large blue and white "L".

'Oh crumbs!' Archie exclaimed. He wasn't sure if he was happy or even more frightened. 'I didn't even notice it! What do you think it means?' he asked.

'I have no idea,' Flora stated.

Archie could hardly speak. His heart was thundering and his palms felt sweaty. The sight of the letter "L" alarmed him even more because it now made what had happened to him very real.

Flora saw the look on his face.

'Sit down before you fall down,' she ordered. Then she sat on the rug next to him.

'Okay, so you've definitely been haunted, that's obvious but by haunting standards I don't think it was too bad. It wasn't an over the top, scary film type of haunting. It could've been a lot worse and an awful lot scarier.'

Archie raised his eyebrows.

'Well alright, it is scary but really it's quite good for us. Now we know that someone is trying to send us a message.' She looked at the "L" again. 'We need to do some detective work.'

Archie nodded.

'We should make a list then do some research.'

Archie nodded again.

'We can't do that here. Let's meet at my house after school on Monday. I'll go and buy a new notebook and then we can decide what to do next.'

Archie continued to nod.

'I always believed you,' she said, squeezing his hand. 'When you think about it it's actually quite exciting. I've always wanted to be a detective and now I get to have a trial run!'

Archie stared at her but Flora ignored the look. 'So when you get your voice back, I think we should get out of here.' Despite her earlier bravery, she was starting to feel creeped out.

They got up quickly.

Archie spoke at last. 'Do you reckon it's a *real* ghost?'

Flora was nodding now.

'Spooky eh?' and he suddenly grinned. They both started to giggle, quietly at first and then their giggles turned into laughter.

'I don't know why I'm laughing,' Archie said, 'I'm scared to death!'

The passage didn't seem quite as dark as they made their way along it to the stairs. Although she didn't mention it to Archie, Flora thought she saw movement from the corner of her eye – a tendril of light in the gloomy space – but when she turned her head to look, there was nothing there.

CHAPTER TEN

Since her papa had returned, Harriet could not believe how different she felt. Every morning she hurried out of bed without being called twice, she even enjoyed the lessons with her governess.

She had missed her father but she had not realised quite how much. She felt like a different person, free of the misery that used to settle upon her. Even her mama, usually cool and distant, was smiling more and although she still scolded Harriet, the telling off was never as harsh.

Aside from the mornings spent with her governess which remained set in stone, there seemed to be little routine to her life anymore, which was a happy wonder to Harriet.

They took afternoon tea outside on warm sunny days, something that they had never done when Papa had been away. He seemed to have a gentle influence over her mother, who had become agreeable to all his advice.

Her mama and papa sat and drank their tea at the pretty wrought iron table on the terrace, chatting and watching Harriet as she and skipped and played hoops in the garden and her mama no longer fussed about her using a parasol. Her papa made her a swing and hung it from the branches of the apple tree, and she used it every day. She took Lily into the garden to show her the swing and Lily pushed her back and forth. Taking a turn, Lily had shrieked with delight when Harriet pushed her higher and higher into the air.

There were lots more visitors too and the house had never been so busy. Lily spent a lot of her time polishing the floor in the hallway, a job that Harriet did not envy.

Papa was not a ship's Captain yet; her mama had said that would only be a matter of time, but his position as an officer on the *Beagle* had allowed him and Mr Darwin to become friends and he was one of the visitors that often called at their home.

One of the most exciting things about Papa's return however, was the luggage that he had brought back with him, not his uniforms and clothing – but the collection of items in two large, battered tin trunks.

One trunk now resided in his study, Harriet's favourite room in their house. The room was lined with dark oak panelling and tall mahogany bookshelves that held the most wonderful bound books, there was a metal ladder attached to the shelves that Harriet and her papa used to slide along the walls to reach the books at the very top.

On the floor in the centre of the room, a dark red Persian rug with tasselled ends, a purchase from a journey her papa had made before she was born, gave the room an exotic, spicy smell.

His oak desk stood in one corner and was always neatly arranged with quills, ink pens, paper and an inkwell. Harriet liked to sit in the cracked leather chair and pretend she was the prime minister or sometimes the new queen, going about her duties for the good of the country.

The trunk was tied with two large buckles and when her papa first returned home, Harriet could not wait to open it – but her papa had other ideas.

'This is the trunk I have filled with things for you,' he had said pointing at the smaller of the two, 'I think that its contents would be far too much to absorb if I were to open it and pull out everything at once. You would quickly forget where each item came from and its purpose. So I have been thinking that we will play a game. We shall keep it in my study and remove something from it each week so that you can look at it, learn something about it and perhaps even use it. That way you will also learn about the country it came from and we can study the world together.'

Harriet had been disappointed by his idea, though she would not have dared to say so.

Then her papa had smiled at her. 'Don't look so crestfallen, my dear. It will be a great game. Do not forget that I have had many years to think about what to collect for you and think how exciting it will be, like a birthday every week!'

Harriet had liked *that* idea and the more she'd thought about it, the more she had come around to it. She would receive a new gift regularly and she could spend time learning about it with her papa instead of her governess.

'Also, the other trunk can be opened immediately as it holds some items for both you and your mama,' he smiled again. 'Now how does that sound?'

Harriet went to him and hugged him before she ran from the room calling to her mama to come quickly.

The items in the first trunk did not disappoint. They were the most delightful things – bolts of brightly coloured silks, which they would send to be made into beautiful dresses, and white cotton thread that had been sewn into delicate lace cloths for their dressing tables. He had brought spices for Cook to use in the kitchen and some, in small pouches, for Harriet to hang in her wardrobe to scent her clothing. There were two huge sun bleached shells from remote, deserted beaches, that made her imagine the soft sand as clean as the pure snow that her papa talked about. He'd brought back a small decorative wrought iron ship, a replica of the *Beagle*, crafted in South America, it had been made the same way that a blacksmith shapes metal for horses' hooves, and which, he said, could be attached to an outside wall. 'To always remind me of my incredible journey,' he had told Harriet.

The *Beagle* had taken him to many wonderful places.

After setting sail from Plymouth, his first stop was at some islands off the west coast of Africa called the Canary Islands. She imagined them to be pretty and small like the little yellow birds but her papa said they were islands made up of dark grey rocks with shores of black sand!

They had sailed on and crossed the equator and reached South America where they stopped at Brazil then on to Argentina and to the Falkland Islands at the bottom tip of South America. He had explained that after much fighting with the Argentineans the Falkland Islands now belonged to Britain, though he said it was a barren, desolate place that he could never imagine being colonised no matter how long it belonged to us.

They continued to Chile and experienced an earthquake which he said was worse than the most terrible of storms he had ever experienced at sea. Then they moved on to the Galapagos Islands. There they remained for two months and he told Harriet that it was a place full of strange and captivating creatures unlike anything she would ever have seen. Mr Darwin had spent a lot of time studying the birds, animals and reptiles, including the giant tortoises on the Galapagos. Harriet had seen small tortoises but could not imagine them being giant, as big as boulders her papa said, and with faces that looked like toothless old men.

Their journey took them to New Zealand and Australia, the Cocos Islands, Mauritius and the southern point of Africa before returning to Argentina. From there they had finally sailed for England. Harriet was exhausted just finding the countries on her papa's globe. No wonder they had taken five years to reach home.

Her papa said that Mr Darwin had spent much of the time studying the plants and animals as well as the places that they visited, and that he had collected important information on all of them. Harriet thought it to be the most exciting thing she had ever heard. She would have given anything to have seen all that he had described.

The promise of the other gifts made her even more excited. She knew that whatever items her father had chosen and placed in the "gift" trunk were going to be very special, and a small part of her wished she hadn't agreed to his plan of only opening it just once each week!

CHAPTER ELEVEN

Much to Archie's amusement, Flora had set up an incident room in her bedroom. She'd found an old blackboard in the garden shed, dusted off the cobwebs and bought some chalks. She had her laptop on her desk, a new notebook, pens and luminous post-it notes.

'Crumbs!' Archie exclaimed as he flung himself down on her bed, 'This place looks like Scotland Yard,' he teased.

'There's no need to be sarcastic,' Flora said grumpily. 'This is all for you really. You want to find out the reason why you were haunted, don't you?'

Archie felt guilty for mocking her, 'Yeah. I'm sorry. It's great, really it is Flora. In fact it's amazing. You must be the most organised person I know. So what have we got so far?'

'Okay,' Flora said forgiving him. 'I've been thinking about questions we need to ask? At the centre of everything is the tile floor, so that's where we need to start. I've got two questions.' She glanced at her notepad. 'Where did the tile floor come from? And how old is it?'

'What about the letter L?' Archie asked.

'I've been thinking about that too and I'm hoping that once we know the origins of the floor that will lead us to what the letter L stands for, and if it doesn't we'll have to ask different questions.'

'We already know that the floor came from a place in March Lane but we don't know where March Lane is. Did you get the catalogues from your dad?'

'Yes they're here.' She grabbed a large tatty cardboard box from underneath her desk and slid it across the bedroom carpet to Archie. 'These are from dad's store cupboard. He's got them set up alphabetically, so I chose the first box of Ms, for March Lane. We'll have to go through them together.'

Archie picked up a book that lay on the top of about ten. It was A4 size and had a hard black cover. A sticky label said M on the front with a date, *2001*. He opened it to the first page and saw that the book had columns, each one with a handwritten heading.

'It's a bit of a daunting job. The catalogues go right back to when my great-grandfather started the business. Everything that came into the warehouse, the item, date, age, its condition and where it came from is written in the different columns.'

'How many books are there exactly?' Archie said, already knowing there would be a lot.

Flora smiled half-heartedly '...well there's a book for each letter of the alphabet and the year, and the business has been going since nineteen eighteen – so that's...'

'...ninety-five years,' Archie interrupted her, he couldn't resist a mathematical problem, 'which means... twenty-six letters of the alphabet multiplied by ninety-five years... that's two thousand four hundred and seventy books!' Archie was shaking his head, 'It'll take us ninety-five years just to go through them!' he said, completely discouraged.

'No, no,' Flora said, 'we can just take the books with the letter M on them from each year. Sometimes there aren't any M's at all. It's still a lot of books but they aren't all full.'

'How many?' Archie asked.

'One hundred and eighty-seven,' said Flora with a sigh. She saw the look on Archie's face, 'I know it won't be exciting ploughing through a load of dusty old ledgers but police work is about finding clues. Sometimes you have to do the boring stuff before you get to the good.'

'Yeah, I suppose you're right,' Archie said, still unconvinced but relieved that they weren't going to be searching through *thousands* of ledgers, 'and I suppose it will be quite interesting to see some of the really old books.'

'My dad says we've got to be careful with them because the ledgers are antiques themselves.'

Archie considered the box at his feet, 'So this is the first of how many boxes?'

'Um… eighteen,' Flora said and Archie grimaced. 'We may as well make a start and cross our fingers the information we need is in the Ms!'

Archie pulled all the books from the box, kept *2007* to *2015* and gave the rest to Flora.

He said, 'We know it wasn't a recent purchase because your dad said he couldn't remember the tiles and he's pretty good at remembering what comes in, but we may as well look through the newest ledgers, in case he was wrong or we miss something. It would be awful to wade through all the books just to find it was in these all along.'

'I was thinking the same.' She gave him a pen and some post-it notes. 'Anything interesting, write it down and stick it to the front of the ledger. We'll have a review when we stop for a break.'

'Okay,' he smiled as he threw himself onto the floor. Flora joined him.

'Before we start though did you do a search for March Lane on the Internet?' he asked still hopeful.

'Yes of course I did,' she smiled.

'How many hits did you get?'

'Two hundred and sixty-one million. There's loads of March Lanes' and if we don't have the name of a town it's no good.'

'What about in this area?'

'There's a March Lane on the Ciddy housing estate but it was built in 2009.'

Archie opened the first book and said 'Two hundred and sixty-one million! One hundred and eighty-seven doesn't sound so bad now!'

They sat with their backs against the radiator and began their search for clues.

CHAPTER TWELVE

The opening of Harriet's trunk had indeed been special and as each week passed something more exciting was revealed. Her papa had obviously thought carefully about the things he had brought home for her and she had been dazzled and amazed by all of the gifts.

The first item came from the Canary Islands, her papa's first stop on his journey around the world – it was a rock! Harriet would never have believed that she could *ever* be excited about a rock – but it was unlike anything she had ever seen. It was larger than her papa's hand but surprisingly weighed virtually nothing; like holding a feather. He had explained that it was called pumice, and that it had trillions of tiny air pockets inside it which made it light. It had been created when it was thrown from the centre of an erupting volcano! On the revolving globe in his study he showed her precisely where it had come from and, as she held it, she couldn't help feeling awestruck. A little piece of rock that had once lived inside a fiery volcano was now in her possession.

An exquisite bracelet of gold and silver twisted together and finished with a turquoise stone clasp, came out of the trunk on the second week. The bracelet was breath-taking and so unlike the delicate jewellery she had in her jewel box. It had been made in a mining village in Brazil and again they had studied the globe. She put it on each morning and sometimes even wore it to bed. Before she drifted to sleep she thought about the mine deep underground in a continent thousands of miles away, from which the minerals that circled her wrist had come. The bracelet and the volcano rock were placed on her dressing table and they made her feel proud and lucky to own such things.

On the third week her papa produced a parcel wrapped in brown paper. Harriet carefully unfolded it to reveal about forty or fifty tiny black seeds.

'These came from the Galapagos Islands. Do you remember I told you that Mr Darwin studied the birds, animals and reptiles there?'

Harriet nodded.

'These are seeds from one of the plants that the giant tortoises ate. It was a grassy sort of plant and quite tall.'

It was the first time that Harriet had been disappointed although her papa did not seem to notice and continued, 'I thought that you could try to grow the plants from these seeds. They will need a lot of warmth as the weather on the Islands was very hot, so it may be best to start them off in the glass house. Perhaps by growing the plants we could have a little piece of the Galapagos Islands here in our very own garden.'

Harriet liked the idea a little better now that he had mentioned the glass house.

'Will I be allowed to put my hands in the soil?' she

asked. Her mama had never permitted her to go into the glass house.

'Of course you can, you cannot plant anything without getting a little mud under your fingernails can you?' he smiled.

Before her papa had come home she would not have believed that she would be interested in some tiny seeds, no more than her excitement over the volcanic rock. But as she thought about it, she warmed to the idea of planting something and then watching it grow, especially since the species of plant would more than likely be the only one of its kind in the whole of England.

She smiled brightly, 'Thank you, Papa,' she said with much more enthusiasm this time.

'You see, Harriet, the items inside this trunk are not just pretty things. I wanted you to understand where they came from and to learn something from them. I really cannot overstate the value of education. That is one of the most important things I learned when I was away. Perhaps with this knowledge one day you will become a scientist like Mr Darwin,' he said.

Harriet's mouth dropped open, 'A scientist, Papa! Oh that would be wonderful, but can a woman ever become a scientist?' She was astonished that her papa could think such a magnificent thing about her.

'Well we shall have to work on your mama but I cannot see why not. I shall speak to Mr Darwin and ask what his thoughts are. And do not forget our new Queen Victoria, she performs all of her duties just as a King would. Perhaps someday a woman will even become Prime Minister.'

Harriet laughed, 'Papa, now I think you are going too far!'

On her way out of the study she almost fell over Lily, who was on her knees polishing the hallway floor again.

'Oh sorry Lily!' Harriet cried as she stumbled around her.

'Miss Harriet! Are you alright!' Lily exclaimed equally shocked.

'Yes, I'm fine, just as well I didn't drop these,' and she held out the paper package to show her.

'What is it?' Lily said still sitting on her knees.

Harriet crouched down and opened the paper. Lily was unimpressed by the minuscule black seeds that appeared to be a lot like fleas to her.

'They're seeds, another gift from Papa's trunk. He says I am to plant them and watch them grow, and then we will have plants from another continent growing in our garden,' Harriet said brightly.

Lily had no idea what or where another continent was, and she certainly did not like the idea of growing things in the garden with worms and all sorts of other crawly things, but she smiled at Harriet anyway, 'That's lovely, what a nice surprise.'

'It is! Papa has brought the most wonderful presents for me. Things I would never have dreamed would make me so happy.' Then she turned to the staircase and skipped her way up the stairs.

As much as she liked Harriet, Lily thought that she would never understand the upper classes. If her father had brought her back some little black seeds from a trip around the world, she would have told him he could just take them right back to where they came from!

CHAPTER THIRTEEN

A rchie's back was aching and his eyes were straining to read Flora's dad's writing. They had been trawling through the ledgers for hours and he had come up with absolutely nothing.

'I think we need a break,' he said suddenly and his voice made Flora jump.

'Yep you're right,' Flora said getting up and stretching like a cat. 'I'll go and get us some lemonade and biscuits, then we can look at what we've found.'

Archie hadn't found anything but Flora had been scribbling in her notepad with each ledger that she'd picked up. The good news was that they were almost at the end of the box; the bad news was that was only fifteen out of one hundred and eighty seven.

'Only one hundred and seventy-two left to go!' Archie said as Flora came back into the room with two cans of Sprite, some KitKats, Penguins and Twixes on a tray.

'Crumbs!' Archie said, 'Your dad got shares in a chocolate biscuit factory?' he laughed taking a KitKat and running his finger nail along the foil wrapper.

'I know, he's got such a sweet tooth, if I ate the amount of chocolate that he does I'd have *no* teeth.' Flora pulled the ring on the can and took a long slurp.

'Right what have we got?' she asked as she sat herself down crossed legged on the floor opposite him.

'Not a lot really,' he said, feeling as though he'd let her down. 'I didn't find anything from March Lane in any of my books. The way these ledgers are set out it's not just where they come from that starts with M, it's also any items that start with the letter M too. Your dad really needs to invest in putting this stuff onto a database. Imagine how much easier it would be if all we had to do...' Archie stopped, he didn't want to sound like he was moaning and upset Flora so he picked up a Twix and unwrapped it.

'Yeah, I'm going to speak to him about that. So ask me what I found,' Flora was grinning.

'Okay, *Sherlock*, what did you find?' Archie said crossing his fingers theatrically.

'I found six items that relate to a March Lane!'

Archie could hardly believe their luck, 'Was one of them the tile floor?'

'Um... no,' Flora said and Archie's heart sank.

'But listen to this and tell me what you think,' Flora picked up her notepad. 'In April 2000, a builder called D Pringle brought in a Victorian fireplace, twenty pieces of bevelled mahogany skirting boards and a double Belfast sink, which my dad bought from him and which he'd noted *"came from a property – 1 March Lane, Romstone"*. Then in June 2000, the same builder brought in three chimney pots from the same property. That's it,' Flora said.

'Well it's a start,' Archie said, 'at least it means we have a house number and a town for March Lane – although it mightn't be the same house that the tiles came from.'

'I know, and the tiles weren't Victorian, I think they were older than that. My dad didn't remember March Lane either but then he was trying to relate it to tiles and it was fifteen years ago.'

'So what do we do next?' Archie asked.

'Before we look at another box of ledgers let's see how far away this March Lane in Romstone is,' said Flora.

Archie would've been happy never to look at another ledger again. 'Good idea,' he said as he got up.

He sat at the laptop on Flora's desk. Using Google maps he typed in directions to March Lane, Romstone, 'Says it's forty-one point six miles away. There's no street view though.'

'That's a shame, we could've checked the age of the house. It's a bit out of the way but we could probably get my dad to take a drive there next Sunday.'

'I'm sure he would but how are we going to explain why we want to go there?'

'I'll tell him it's for a history project and that the tile floor got me thinking about what sort of house it came from, which is a sort of half-truth.'

'Has he asked to see the floor yet?'

'No I think he's forgotten about it. He's been so busy with his bookwork that it's probably the last thing on his mind.'

'Won't this remind him though? What if he asks to see it? We can't very well show him the heap of broken bits, can we.'

'Don't worry about my dad, he'll be fine. You know I hate lying to him too but it's only a little fib really and once we know more perhaps we can tell him what's going on.'

Archie didn't like the idea of trying to explain to Flora's dad that he'd been haunted by a ghost who had then destroyed the tile floor. He hoped it wouldn't come to that.

'Alright, so we'll print out these directions and you can ask your dad about taking us there next Sunday.'

'Okay. To be honest I couldn't face another four hours of searching these old books,' Flora sighed, 'being a detective is harder than I imagined, I really hope this leads us somewhere.'

'Thinking exactly the same myself,' Archie said. 'If we're done for now, how about putting the Xbox on so that I can beat you at FIFA again?'

Flora smiled, 'Yeah right. Fancy a bet on that?'

'Yep. I bet you two Twixes and a Penguin,' said Archie as he reached for the TV remote.

CHAPTER FOURTEEN

Lily had been sent upstairs to clean Harriet's room and lay the grate ready for the evening's fire; one of the household tasks that she enjoyed.

She put her small wicker basket of paper and sticks on the hearth, took the cloth and tin of wax from her apron pocket and went over to the dressing table. Lily picked up the rock that weighed almost nothing and examined it closely. Harriet had explained to her where it had come from and just like Harriet, Lily liked the idea that it had once been inside a burning volcano.

Lily inspected the small parcel of seeds. Harriet had been thrilled about the thought of planting them – but although she could understand why she was excited about the volcano rock, Lily still didn't know what the fuss for gardening was about. She'd helped her dad grow vegetables in the tiny back yard at home since she was little and she'd never liked it one bit. It was always difficult getting the mud from under her nails and she hated worms like no other creature on earth. Still, she wasn't going to spoil Harriet's excitement.

The bed was a tangle of sheets, blankets and pillows which she smoothed out, tucked in and plumped up. She moved around the room picking up clothes and books from the floor. She sorted the clean dresses and petticoats from the dirty and put the clean ones on the bed ready to hang in the wardrobe. She hated the wardrobe almost as much as she hated worms. It was too large and creaky and she thought that at any minute something might jump out from it. Even though she knew that she was being stupid letting her imagination take over, it was the only thing that spoiled her enjoyment of being in Harriet's room.

When she had finished the tidying and polishing and had laid the sticks and paper in the grate, she finally built up the courage and carrying the dresses, she went to the wardrobe.

As she nervously opened the dark wood doors, a waft of the spices that the master had brought home from his travels reached her. It was certainly nicer than the smell of mothballs. She quickly began to hang the dresses onto the silk hangers. Just as she was about to close the doors Lily noticed something on the bottom shelf tucked amongst the shoes. Delving in and hastily pulling her hand back out she saw that she was holding Harriet's diary, usually kept on the dressing table. She must have hidden it in the wardrobe to prevent the mistress from reading it, which could only mean that she had written something that she did not want the mistress to see.

Lily was tempted to open it. The book felt hot in her hands, but she kept a diary and would have been horrified if someone ever got hold of hers and read it. She blushed at the thought and quickly returned the book to its hiding place. Harriet told her most of her secrets anyway. They were friends, despite what the mistress thought and she would certainly not snoop through her friend's feelings. If there was anything to tell, Harriet would confide in her in good time but Lily would mention how easily Harriet's mama might have found it, if she'd opened the wardrobe.

She closed the doors tightly just as Harriet came into the room.

'Oh! You startled me,' said Harriet as she saw Lily standing by the wardrobe.

'I was just putting some of your dresses away.'

'I'm sorry, Lily. I meant to pick them up myself,' Harriet said guiltily.

'Miss Harriet, can I say something?'

'Of course you can, you know you can say anything you like to me. You are just about my one and only friend,' Harriet smiled.

'Alright. Well, when I was putting your clothes away I came across this,' Lily grimaced as once again she opened the doors and took out the diary.

'Oh no!' Harriet cried, 'You didn't read it did you?' Her cheeks flushed scarlet.

'Of course not,' said Lily rushing towards her. 'I would never do such a thing. It's your own world inside this little book. I only told you because your mama would have found it as easily as I did.'

Harriet slumped to the floor and Lily sat down with her.

'Lily. You know me too well. I *was* hiding it from Mama. Am I a terrible daughter?'

'Don't be daft, there is no way I would want my mam

to read my diary. She'd have a fit and turn blue,' said Lily smiling.

Harriet smiled too, 'Well, if Mama read what I have written recently she would have a fit and turn blue too!' and she began to laugh. Then both girls were giggling.

When they finally stopped Lily said, 'I have an idea. Why don't you ask Joseph if he will make you a little draw big enough to hold your diary? One that will fit inside the bottom of the wardrobe. A secret compartment.'

Harriet giggled again, 'That's a wonderful idea but how will I explain that to Mama?'

'Don't be silly, Harriet. He'll have to do without your parents knowing.'

Harriet was shocked that anyone would do anything in the house without her mother or father's permission. 'Do you think he would?'

Lily nodded, 'Yes. He's really handy is Joe and he would be tickled by the thought of doing something secretive. He's only a couple of years older than us. I'm sure he would do it if I ask him.'

'But can we can trust him not to say anything?

'I know we can,' Lily said.

'Really?'

'He's a nice lad and kind-hearted too. I'll have a word with him and explain the situation when he comes to do the garden in the morning. Everyone deserves a little bit of privacy – even us,' said Lily.

'Lily you have saved me from a host of terrible questions from Mama and if the secret drawer works, then

I won't ever have to worry about her prying eyes again.'

'You might have to tell your mama that you have misplaced your diary, so that she doesn't wonder where it is.'

Harriet stopped for a moment, 'Oh... but what if Joseph gets caught?'

'Then we'll just have to make sure he doesn't. He'll have to come and measure up, go away and make it, then come back to fit it. He's always in and out of the house doing jobs for Mr Wickes and your papa. He'll like the challenge of it, I'm sure. And if he doesn't want to do it, I know that he won't breathe a word to anyone. He's as good as gold and no fool. Leave it to me.'

Harriet hesitated but only for a second, 'Alright then... ask him, but if he says no you must make him promise not to tell.'

'I will,' said Lily.

'If I tell you what was so important that I did not want Mama to know, will you make me an honest promise never to tell another living soul?'

Lily put her hand on her heart and said solemnly, 'You have my word as your friend.'

So Harriet told her.

CHAPTER FIFTEEN

'I think this is the turning,' Flora said, reading the map. The three of them were in her dad's van, Flora was navigating. She'd persuaded him to take them on a Sunday afternoon drive to Romstone.

Earlier that morning she had explained that they'd finally found March Lane in the old ledgers, but that there'd been no record of the tile floor. She'd told him that she was still interested in finding out a little more about the type of house that the floor might have come from for a history project at school.

It was only a small fib but Flora still felt guilty about telling him half-truths, thankfully her dad had agreed and she hadn't had to deceive him any further.

They turned into March Lane, a narrow gravel lane with high beech hedges on both sides.

'I hope we don't meet any traffic,' her dad said. 'There's no passing places. We'd have to reverse all the way back.'

But ten minutes later, not having met any cars or passed any houses, they emerged at a dead end blocked by a large wooden farm gate. They could go no further.

On their right, bordered by a low-cut beech hedge, was a beautiful double fronted Georgian house – the only property on March Lane.

Flora's stomach did an excited somersault. 'Well it's the right age,' she said.

Her dad parked the van against the hedge and they all got out.

'Oh this is so... grand,' said Flora quietly.

The house was three stories high. Built from red brick, it had obviously been restored with great care. The white front door at its centre stood between two tall Georgian windows. On the second floor were a further three windows with two smaller windows tucked into the roof above them. White painted pillars were situated on either side of the front door, topped with a triangular portico. A small, wrought iron ship that might have belonged to a pirate, sailed above it. A delicate white picket gate opened onto a terracotta tile path that led to the front door.

As the three of them were stood in front of the house, a lady opened the door. Wearing grey cords, green wellies and an oversized tatty red jumper that swamped her petite frame, she appeared to be in her mid fifties; her shoulder length grey hair was brushed gently away from her face, which was delicate and pixie-like. She held a pair of secateurs in her hand.

'Can I help you?' she asked abrasively.

'Sorry. Yes, sorry. We seem to be staring at your house. You must be wondering what on earth we're doing?' her dad was flustered that they'd been caught.

The woman's voice softened as she nodded, 'Well yes, I was quite.'

'I'm sorry, shall I start again?' Her dad smiled. 'My

name is Horace Theodore, this is my daughter Flora and her friend Archie,' Flora waved, feeling stupid. 'We were in the area because my daughter is doing a project. A history project. And your house, it's of some interest to her.'

The lady hesitated for a moment. 'Well... You had better come in then. Close the gate behind you and follow me,' she said brusquely, and with that she walked along a stone path past the windows and disappeared around the side of the house.

The three of them looked at each other in surprise and then her dad quickly opened the gate.

CHAPTER SIXTEEN

L ily raced up the stairs from the kitchen to greet the newly arrived visitor and found Mr Darwin in the hallway with Mr Wickes.

'Hello, Lily,' said Mr Darwin. He smiled sadly at her and passed her his hat and coat.

'Good evening, sir,' Lily took his things to the hallway cupboard.

'The master is in his study, sir,' she heard Mr Wickes say. She peered around the door as Mr Darwin followed him.

Mr Darwin didn't look himself again. He was usually quite jolly and often teased Lily about her hair falling out of its pins, but over the past few weeks when he had visited it seemed as though his cheerfulness had disappeared and instead, had been replaced by anxiety which showed on his pale face.

It had been over two years since the master had returned home and life at the house had grown into a steady pace of normality once again. He was a kind person to work for and Lily was very content. But she knew that he was planning his next voyage. Harriet had cried when she had been told and Lily had comforted her. The master was not sailing for almost a year yet, and only for a short time; he would be away for just three months and Lily had told Harriet to take some comfort from that. He had to work and there was no denying that the sea was in his blood, he could not be contained on land forever.

But something was wrong. Lily could sense it. She had seen it in Mr Darwin's face and had also felt it in the demeanour of the master, who was preoccupied with his thoughts most of the time. Harriet had noticed it too and had confided in Lily that she believed her papa was missing the sea. Lily had agreed but she thought that it was something more. The master seemed fearful. She knew that something was *very* wrong.

She wasn't sure why she did it, but when Mr Wickes made his way back downstairs she pretended to be fussing over the coats and then she slipped quietly along the hallway to the study. The door was slightly ajar. Her head was urging her not to but she just could not stop herself. She put her ear to the opening.

The voices inside were muffled and she could only pick out a few words, unsure who they belonged to. Her heart was pounding.

'Impossible to say...'

'But... findings are correct... experiments...'

'Extreme danger... people... snooping...'

'Dreadful trouble... your family... this household...'

'Must... leave...'

'Dies down...'

The voices suddenly got closer and she scurried away from the door just as it opened. Running on her toes along the corridor she dived into the hallway cupboard hoping that she had not been seen. It would be the end of her job if she was caught.

'Let us decide what to do tomorrow, Charles. I fully understand the urgency, and the longer you leave it the more serious it may become.'

'It is not safe and yes, you are right, William, but I assure you, everything we have spoken about is true. I am disturbed by this turn of events and very concerned for you and your family. I can hardly sleep at night it is troubling me so much,' Mr Darwin said quietly.

'I will have a think. Come back at ten o'clock tomorrow night and we will make a plan,' the master said, his voice a dull whisper.

'My hat and coat,' Mr Darwin said.

Lily's heart thundered. She quickly tucked herself underneath some long winter coats that were on hooks at the back, she prayed that the master would not notice her legs and feet sticking out at the bottom. She was in luck, he continued to talk in a hushed tone as he took Mr Darwin's things from the stand at the front of the cupboard. She had not been found out.

Lily heard the front door open and close and the master's footsteps retreating into his study. She breathed a sigh of relief then cautiously poked her head around the door before hastily making her way back down the stairs.

Cook was sitting at the long wooden table in the kitchen, drinking her last cup of tea of the evening. She could hear Mr Wickes in the pantry.

'Pot's still warm if you want one,' Cook said, thankfully not noticing how long Lily had been upstairs.

'No thanks, Cook. I'll get to bed if there's nothing you want doing.'

'You go on up, girl. I'll be right behind you after I've drunk me tea.'

Lily took the back staircase up to the servants' rooms at the top of the house. There were three rooms in the roof space and hers was the smallest. Still, she didn't mind that, when she'd lived at home she'd had to share a bed with three of her sisters, so a space all to herself was a real luxury.

She undressed, put on her nightgown and crawled into the narrow single bed. As she lay there her mind went over what she had heard downstairs. Mr Darwin and the master sounded like they were in trouble. And after the short bursts of conversation she had heard, she had the impression that it had something to do with their journey together. Whatever it was, they were in danger because of it, and it was not only the master that was in jeopardy but the whole household: Harriet, the mistress, Cook and Mr Wickes. The worry pressed down on her chest and almost made it hard to breathe. What if the family were at risk and she had known and done nothing? "Extreme danger": they were not words that were used lightly. If only there was something she could do, but how could she? She was just a housemaid.

She stared into the darkness for a long time. If she could just find out what was going on, even given her low status she *might* still be able to help. It would mean risking her job, but perhaps it would be worth the risk. Although she really liked her job, she loved the family more – and would do anything for them.

Sleep did not come easily and when it did, she found herself in a nightmare where she was running from shadows and coats that had only legs and no people inside them.

When she finally woke still weary in the grey early morning light, she believed that what she was going to do would be the right thing.

CHAPTER SEVENTEEN

The back of the house was as lovely as the front. Two sets of French doors opened onto an old stone patio that ran its entire width. The patio was fronted by mature lavender bushes which had been pruned hard ready for winter. Steps led down to an expanse of lawn, half the size of a football pitch, which had grown so long that it was more like a field of pale wheat. Behind the lawn was a small apple and plum tree orchard, the trees ripe with their autumn fruit. In the furthest corner stood a large greenhouse, its glass dirty and mossy. Just visible in the distance was the top of a willow tree which had lost most of its leaves.

The garden seemed to lack some care. It was large and mature with shrubs and bushes and pampas grasses creating a patchwork effect, though most of them were dying now that it was autumn.

The whole garden was surrounded by a high old red brick wall. Trellis was attached to the walls and the bare branches of climbing plants lay against them in a spider's web of tangles.

Flora thought that despite its unkempt air it was still the most beautiful garden she had ever seen. She could only imagine how wonderful it would look in summer.

Outside one set of French doors a plastic patio table and chairs were heaped with several buckets full of apples.

The woman was waiting for them.

'My name is Mable Evans,' she said in the same abrupt way, 'introductions over. So before I give you a history lesson about the house, grab a bucket and follow me.' She picked up a tin pail and marched off across the lawn.

Fortunately Flora had worn her walking boots and old Sunday clothes. Her dad and Archie were stood open-mouthed in front of her.

'Jump to it,' she said laughing quietly, and taking an orange plastic bucket from beside the table she quickly followed Mable.

Flora could hear Archie and her father laughing too as they trooped behind her and, when they reached the orchard, she saw several ancient wooden ladders propped against the tree trunks. Mable was already climbing one, 'Flora you can pick the plums; you too, Archie, is it? And Horace, start on the cooking apples at the back.'

Like three small children they obeyed Mable's orders and climbed the ladders dutifully. They spent the next two hours quietly collecting their respective fruit and Flora enjoyed every moment. The autumn sunlight warmed her face as she reached into the delicate branches of the tree. The smell of sweet fruit surrounded her in a haze of plum perfume. She had never done anything like it before, but she felt that she could do it for hours and never get fed up. When her bucket was full, she climbed down; Archie, her dad and Mable were already making their way back to the house. She charged after them, lugging the heavy bucket with her.

When she got back to the patio the low sun was still touching the back of the house and her dad and Archie were sat down.

'Mable's gone to make a cup of tea.' Her dad smiled and his face was rosy and shining like she hadn't seen in a long time. Even Archie's usually pale face had some colour in his cheeks. He was eating a plum.

Flora plonked herself down onto a patio chair and closed her eyes as she enjoyed the last rays before the cold chill of the evening took hold.

Mable returned with four mugs of tea on a tray. Saying nothing, she went back into the house, reappearing with five Tupperware tubs in her arms which she placed on the table. She went inside a third time and came back with plates and forks.

'May as well see what the *fruits* of your labours will produce, pardon the pun. All homemade too,' she said more sincerely this time as she opened the tubs.

There was a cake in each. But they weren't *just* cakes, they were masterpieces! A plum and spiced apple cake, an apple and blackberry cake sprinkled with cinnamon, a plum jam cake dusted with icing sugar, an apple preserve turnover topped with crystallised sugar and an "iced plum delight," as Mable called it. It was cake heaven and without a word, all four of them set about demolishing the spread as if they had never eaten before.

When they were full, and all suffering from a sugar-fruit

overload, Mable stood up and said, 'Come on, let's go inside. It'll get too cold to sit out once the sun disappears. I've lit the fire and it'll be nice and warm in there. Don't worry about the dishes, I'll get those later.'

Flora was astonished. Mable was now talking to them as if they were old friends. Trooping obediently after her, they found themselves in a large open kitchen. There was an AGA cooker against the wall, which made the room feel like an oven itself, and a huge battered pine kitchen table in the centre, above which hung copper pots and pans of all sizes. They followed Mable to the front of the house into a large but surprisingly cosy study. The walls were lined with bookshelves and there were two long, soft sofas and an armchair taking up most of the room, all of them angled to face a fire roaring in the grate. Flora, Archie and her dad sat on the sofas whilst Mable took the armchair.

'Before we get started I'd just like to thank you for your help. I was wondering how on earth I was going to get those fruit trees done today. It's so late in the season and there is nothing worse than seeing fruit rotting on the ground. I usually have a man come round and help with the fruit harvest and the gardening, Mr Pryce from the village, but he's been taken poorly and won't be back until the spring.' She smiled at them.

Flora was amazed for a second time. Not only had Mable's sternness disappeared but her voice had changed to a rich soft tone with an accent she couldn't quite place. Her face had changed too, the glower had been replaced with an easy, gentle smile that suited her delicate features.

Flora suddenly decided that she could grow to like Mable a lot!

'Well it was a bit of a surprise,' said Flora's dad with a laugh.

'But in a good way,' Flora said hoping that they might be asked to help again.

'Right, now I shall repay you for your good deed. What was it you wanted to know about the house? I think I have just what you might need.' She stood up and went to one of the shelves pulling out a large book with a green leather cover.

'This is a photograph album that I inherited with the house.' She gave it to Flora who waited before she opened it.

'Have you always lived here, Mable?' she asked.

'Oh no, I only bought it in 2006. It belonged to a Mr and Mrs Morgan before that. They were an older couple and were hoping to move away to a warmer climate. I'd just come back from abroad and wanted to buy a house in Romstone. I lived in this area when I was a girl. Mr and Mrs Morgan bought it from a builder who had ripped out almost every original feature; a tragedy in a house like this. How he got away with it I just don't know. It's a listed building,' she said sadly.

'That will be Pringle, the builder I bought the fireplace from,' said Flora's dad.

'I'm sorry. I don't understand,' Mable said.

'I'm sorry too. We haven't really explained how and why we came to be here,' said Flora's dad.

'Well I'm not sure I gave you a chance,' Mable smiled.

Flora's dad smiled back, 'I own a reclamation and salvage business in Vale. Pringle brought some things in from a property in March Lane back in 2000 and I bought them from him. He must have been renovating this place. Don't get me wrong, Mable, I would never have bought anything had I known it was taken from a listed property.'

'Oh I see. That's good,' said Mable with a nod.

'Well it all started with Flora finding the floor. You tell Mable, Flora,' said her dad.

Flora needed to be careful about her story. She didn't want to let the real reason out or embarrass Archie who was sitting quietly besides her.

'I was helping my dad. Archie and I were sorting out the tile room and we came across a floor, a red tile floor with pretty blue and white flowers. It might be Victorian or Georgian. The label on the crate said March Lane. We have to do a history project on local buildings, so I thought it would be nice to try and find the house that the floor belonged to. We looked through Dad's old ledgers and found an entry for March Lane but it wasn't a tile floor, it was a Victorian fireplace, some skirting board, a sink and some chimney pots. That was the builder my dad was talking about.'

Mable seemed thoughtful.

'We just thought it would be nice to link the tiles to an actual house,' Archie said and Flora could feel him willing her not to give their secret away.

'Well I did think that the wood flooring in the hall was

a later addition, come and see,' Mable said getting up again. They all walked into the hallway. The floor was a marmalade orange, wood block, a little wobbly in places. Flora's dad crouched down.

'You're right, I don't think this is the original floor, wood block was usually put in later – what date was the house built, Mable? Do you know?'

They went back to the warmth of the fire.

'It was built around the 1820s. It's Georgian but it would have had some Victorian bits and pieces added like fireplaces, pelmets and skirting boards. It's the same today we modernise our homes as we go along. A hundred years ago, if people could afford it they would modernise their homes too. That's why it may have had a Victorian fireplace. There's still one in the small attic bedroom, though I don't know how the builders missed it. I found this Georgian fireplace in a reclamation yard, probably like yours, Horace,' she said, nodding towards the fire burning brightly, 'and the kitchen table, which only had the smallest amount of woodworm, was down in the cellar. I think the Morgan's left it behind.'

'You have a cellar?' Archie asked imagining all sorts of nasty things down there.

'Yes,' Mable replied, 'It's where I keep the plums and apples until I'm ready to preserve and cook them. It's nice and cool but in its day it would have been the kitchen, scullery and pantry. This would have been a wealthy family house, not quite upper class with ten or twenty servants but there would probably have been at least three or four people employed by the owner. It has links to the sea too. You might have noticed the ship above the portico outside, I found that when I was digging the vegetable patch by the greenhouse.'

'So you think the tile floor came from this house?' Archie asked Mable.

'Quite possibly. Have a look through that album and I'll see what else I can find. You might need to help me, Horace. I'm a bit short for the top ones,' Mable stood up and Flora's dad followed.

Flora opened the book. It was more like a scrap book than a photograph album. The pages were yellowed and aging and it smelled like musty, damp newspapers.

The first page was a photograph of the house. The paint was peeling from the windows and the roof was sagging in the middle, it was in very poor condition. A date was written underneath, *1994 – 1 March Lane.*

Between them Flora and Archie started to turn the pages and the history of the house unfolded. There were photographs and newspaper cuttings going right back to the start of the 1900s. Some photos were copied from books and some taken from the Internet. There were copies of old deeds and some curling photos of previous owners, of which there were many, from different eras in time. There were notes on families that had come, lived and grown up in it and then moved on. Flora and Archie were absorbed by what they were reading.

'Do you know who made this album, Mable?' Flora asked as she turned the last page.

'I don't, as I said I inherited it with the house. I found it amongst some of the things that were tucked away in one of the bedrooms. Isn't it wonderful? A lot of time obviously went into creating it.'

Flora reluctantly closed the book and stood to put it back on the shelf.

As she did something fell from inside.

Flora thought it was a loose photograph but when she bent to pick it up she realised it was a small ink drawing on a piece of thick cream paper. The size of a small envelope, it was obviously old, like the album. She turned it over; in writing that had almost faded away was a date – *1837.*

She turned it back and peered closely at the drawing. It was a beautifully detailed portrait of a tall man, a lady and a young girl of about fourteen. They were dressed in old-fashioned clothing; the lady and girl were wearing long dresses and the man wore a jacket, jodhpurs and high boots. The three of them were stood at the door of the house. Flora felt a rush of excitement.

'Mable, look at this, did you know this was in the album?' Flora held up the drawing carefully.

Mable came over, took it from her and gasped 'Oh my! I've never seen this before. It's so old!' She was looking at the date on the back. 'This was inside the album?'

'Yes, but we didn't see it on any of the pages, did we Archie?'

'No,' Archie said.

'It just fell out when I stood up. Do you think it's really that old?' Flora asked.

Mable peered at it closely. 'It's so unusual, early portraits were almost always posed in a room or a studio. To be stood outside, in front of the house, well it's probably unheard of. Perhaps the date is wrong but it has the feeling of being very *real,* look at their faces, they seem so… alive. It's a lovely drawing.'

'Do you know who they might be?' Flora asked.

Mable shook her head slowly, 'I can only assume they must have lived here. If the date is to be believed that was only about seventeen years after the house was built, perhaps they were the first owners,' Mable continued to stare at the drawing.

'Mable, look behind the people,' Flora said leaning over her shoulder.

'What is it?' both Archie and her dad asked at the same time.

Mable smiled. 'The detail is amazing for a drawing this old and oh… you can just make out the floor behind them in the hallway, it seems to be tile. Look,' she said, showing the picture to Flora's dad, 'there's no colour but you can see that the floor has got small flowers on it… just like the one that Flora described.'

CHAPTER EIGHTEEN

'Cook,' said Lily pretending to yawn widely. 'I'm really tired tonight, if it's alright with you, do you think I can go up to bed?' Lily was hoping that Cook wouldn't ask her to sit down for a cup of tea. She glanced up at the clock. It was half past nine. She usually didn't go to bed until ten and then only if she wasn't needed to help prepare any veg for the following day, or deal with something for Harriet or the mistress.

Cook was pouring herself a second cup from the pot. It had been a quiet day and she was in a kind mood, 'Yes it's alright girl, you go on up, Mr Wicks will join me in a minute. Oh hang on, 'ave you forgotten? Mr Darwin is visiting tonight, so you'll need to be upstairs to take 'is coat an' hat.'

Lily's heart skipped a beat.

'What's that about Mr Darwin?' Mr Wickes asked as he came into the kitchen and sat down at the long wooden table.

'He's calling tonight remember, quite late, 'bout ten o'clock. The mistress told me when I was upstairs yesterday discussing the weekly menu. Strange time to be calling if you ask me,' said Cook.

'Ah yes, the master has some business to discuss with

him. Mr Darwin has been so busy of late, that tonight was the only convenient time,' said Mr Wickes, pouring a cup of tea. 'Don't you mind, Lily, I'll sort out his hat and coat and wait up for him to leave. You can go to bed now. Anyway it's an early start for you tomorrow, up at four don't forget. You need to let the chimney sweep in and stay with him while he goes about his business. He'll be coming through the back door. Sweep's trustworthy enough, but I never know about those boys he brings with him. Little snipes some of them.'

Cook nodded in agreement. 'Caught one of 'em with his hands in the biscuit tin last time,' she said crossly. 'I'd 'ave given him one anyway but he didn't even ask!'

Lily thanked them both and rushed out of the kitchen to the back stairs before they could change their minds. But instead of making her way up to the third floor, she quietly opened the door onto the second floor landing.

All was dark and quiet as she tiptoed along the oriental carpet runner, hoping that the floorboards wouldn't creak enough to wake Harriet or the mistress. At the far end of the corridor she turned and stealthily made her way back down the front stairs into the hallway. She listened outside the study for a minute. The master was usually in the drawing room at this time having a glass of port and a cigar, so she opened the door quickly and slipped inside.

The room was in darkness and she crept over to the empty trunk in the corner. She undid the buckles, lifted the lid and climbed in. The trunk was small and Lily had to curl up into a tight ball so that she could pull the lid back over her. For a moment she stopped to think about the gravity of what she was doing and she almost climbed back out. If she was caught she knew that it would be the end of her life at the house or any other house for that matter. She would never be trusted again. But as much as that scared her, she needed to know what the master and Mr Darwin were so frightened of. And so she stayed where she was, curled up like a hibernating hedgehog, waiting.

Lily must have dozed off because she was startled when a voice suddenly spoke inside the room, very close to her hiding place.

'Don't wait up, Wickes. I'll show Mr Darwin out when he leaves,' she heard the master say.

'It will only be a quick visit, Wickes. I shan't be too long,' said Mr Darwin.

'Very well, sir, if you're sure. Good night both,' said Mr Wickes.

'Good night.'

The conversation began as soon as the door was closed.

'This is madness Charles, skulking around at this time of the night is just not safe, I should never have suggested it,' said the master quietly.

'I was not followed I am sure of it but I have a feeling my papers have been examined. I believe they sent someone to search my lodgings and I fear because of our friendship we both may be in terrible danger,' said Mr Darwin.

'Yes, I am afraid I agree with you. I have noticed a

strange fellow waiting around at the end of the lane and when I approach he turns quickly and makes off. When I was in town on business yesterday I saw the same chap again. What do you think we should we do, Charles?' asked the master. There was concern in his voice.

'I have come to realise that our society is not yet ready for a discovery such as this. I must gather together all my documentation regarding this particular research and hide it, somewhere safe, where prying eyes will not find it. It must be secreted away until people are ready to fully understand. Times are changing, William – but not fast enough. If my research is taken it could mean disaster for me and, as my confidante, for you also. I am certain this goes much higher than just a group of unsavoury people who wish to know my findings.'

'What do you mean?' asked the master.

'I mean the government, perhaps the church. I am sure that some members of parliament and the high clergy wish to see my demise. I have been unpopular with the recent letters and enquiries I have made in the name of science since our return.

'If this *other* research is found to have the value that I know it does, I will be vilified as the discoverer of the most ungodly thing on this earth. Many will not be able to see its true significance, how important it is. They will only see it as going against God.' Mr Darwin was obviously very distressed.

There was a pause before he continued, 'I am sorry that my association with you has put you at risk too. As I said yesterday, the voyage on the *Beagle* could implicate you in my discovery. Even though I have shared only a small portion of what I have learned with you, I am still concerned for the welfare of your family William.'

'Then we shall have to do something quickly and must divert attention so that they, whoever *they* may be, will not find out what you have discovered. We must cover your tracks. Do you have the papers with you now?' asked the master.

Lily heard Mr Darwin opening a satchel. 'Yes they are here. I dare not leave them out of my sight.'

The master spoke, 'I have an idea. I will take them from you and hide them. I know a place, a merchant's office at the port, where I can put them inside a safe. I am the only key holder. They can remain locked away until such time that you believe it is not dangerous to show what you have learned to the world – if ever that time comes. I will be leaving next year on my voyage to Europe and if the danger is still obvious, then I will take your research with me and leave it in a secure place in one of the countries to which I will be travelling. It will be too difficult for anyone to follow its trail if it is hidden abroad and I can return there to collect your papers after some time has passed.

'I will write ahead to the merchant's offices, and take them there by carriage at the end of this week. Charlotte need only know that I am carrying out some business in preparation for my next voyage. I shall store them safely here until then.'

'Are you sure? I did not intend to burden you with

them. I only carry them so that they will not be stolen from my lodgings,' said Mr Darwin sounding frightened.

'It will only be for a few days, four at the most. This household is far safer than your lodgings, Charles, we can at least ensure that we know everyone that visits here. Besides I have the perfect hiding place where no one will think to look, should anyone try. And on Friday who would question a sailor conducting business at the port?'

'If… you are sure, William,' said Mr Darwin finally conceding.

'I am certain. I am your friend and I am here to help. I understand what you are trying to do. This discovery could be for the good of all men, but I agree, our society is just not ready yet for what you have learned and in the wrong hands it could be a catastrophe.'

Lily heard Mr Darwin and the master walking to the door.

'It is late. I must go. Please keep those notes safe, but if your family is at risk then destroy them! Your life and that of Charlotte and Harriet are far more important. The rest of my research will not be written down and will remain inside my mind where it will be safest. Does Charlotte know anything of this?'

'No, I do not wish to concern her. In a few days there will be no need to tell her. It will be best if we keep this just between us.'

'Yes you are quite right, the fewer people that know the less risk there will be. I will be in touch, but for now it may be wise for me to put some distance between us. I am readying my diaries of the voyage on the *Beagle* for publishing. I hope that it will put those who seek *this* research off the scent. I will call upon you again in a month or so,' said Mr Darwin.

'I agree. People are talking about your *Beagle Journals* with much anticipation, and if nothing emerges about this other research perhaps those that seek it will lose interest. But do not worry, your papers will be out of this house by the end of the week and then we may breathe a little easier,' said the master.

The door was opened and Lily heard the hushed voices move away from her and then the heavy latch of the front door as it was closed. The master walked back into the room and for a terrible moment Lily thought he was going to lift the trunk's lid, but instead she heard him shuffling papers at his desk before he left the room, shutting the door quietly behind him.

She waited a long time to be sure that he would not return before finally pushing the lid open. Every muscle in her body ached and both her feet were terribly cramped, but she didn't linger. She closed the lid and did up the buckles before opening the door quietly then swiftly making her way from the room. She dashed up the main stairway and as quickly and quietly as she could she ran along the second floor landing and flew through the door to the servants' stairs. What Lily didn't notice in her haste was Harriet's head peering around her bedroom door. She was wondering what an earth Lily was doing tearing along the corridor like a scared cat at midnight.

CHAPTER NINETEEN

Flora and Archie had a lot to think about. It was dark by the time they'd finally left the house on March Lane. Mable had made a photocopy of the old drawing for Flora, and had given her her telephone number in case she had any more questions, she had even invited them to come again and help collect the rest of the fruit, to which her dad had happily agreed.

Archie had come back to Flora's house. She had the feeling that he didn't want to go home to his own empty house and, although it was dark, it wasn't too late for them to have a quick catch-up on the afternoon's events.

They were sat on the floor against the warm radiator in her bedroom.

'So, what do you think?' Flora asked Archie.

'Well I think we found the right March Lane but I'm not sure how that can help us with the... ghost,' Archie said, shuddering at the word.

'I think we need to plan what to do next,' she pulled out the portrait from her fleece pocket, 'I reckon we have to find out who these people are.'

'Why them though?' Archie asked. 'You saw how many people have lived in that house just from the album at Mable's and it didn't go back further than the 1900s.

There could be loads more owners and it could be any one of them that are linked to the... you know what... in the warehouse.'

'I know and I can't say why, I just have a feeling. Look at where they are stood – in front of the house.' She passed him the photocopy of the picture, 'and we can actually see the floor in the background. We didn't see it in any of the photos. These are the only people so far that have a connection to it, however small. How strange is that? Think about it. Remember what Mable said – this is an unusual drawing to begin with because it's not in a studio *and* the tile floor in the background has been included! I think it's the clue we've been waiting for, even if it's just a slither of one – call it a detective's intuition,' she said smiling at him.

Archie nodded, 'I suppose you could be right. If it's the only clue we have, we may as well work with it. So what next, Sherlock?'

'Tomorrow, after school we'll go to the library. We need to give this family a name.'

When they arrived at the library the following day, Flora showed her library card and asked the librarian how they could trace the name of a family that lived in Romstone, through the library's records.

The librarian, was a young, happy woman with big, curly ginger hair and eyebrows to match. Her name badge said "Crystal". She wore numerous sparkly slides in her hair, which was such a bright shade of orange that it really didn't need any further adornment.

Crystal explained how to log in to the computers, and suggested that they begin their search through the electoral register.

'If you don't get anywhere with that you can try the census database. I'll show you how to access that if you don't have any joy,' she said brightly, writing down a password on a slip of paper which she passed across the counter to Flora.

'Have fun!'

'Thanks,' Flora said, and they went up to the computer suite on the second floor.

Logging on to the electoral database was easy. But they didn't have any luck. The database went all the way back to 1839 but the names and addresses were inconsistent and they couldn't find March Lane in Romstone. Flora left Archie and went back downstairs to the librarian.

Five minutes later all three of them were sat in front of the computer.

'That's the problem with the electoral register; it's only really since the end of the Second World War that it's precise enough. I didn't realise you were trying to find anything so far back. We'll try the census I think. The earliest date for that is 1801 and it's been collected every ten years since then, although the first four censuses were merely headcounts so... anyway I'll log you in and you can have a look.'

When she'd gone Archie asked, 'Shall I take a turn? I'll scroll through and you keep your eye out too.'

They spent a long time scanning the old census

archives. They tried the date closest to 1837, the date that had been written on the back of the drawing. There was nothing listed for 1841 and nothing for 1851, so they went back to the beginning. In 1831 they were finally lucky.

1831
1 March Lane, Romstone
Occupiers: 3
Servants: 2

The names of the occupiers were listed:

William Mathias – voter
Charlotte Mathias
Harriet Mathias
Servants: D Wickes (voter), A Parsonage

Archie felt a shiver gallop along his spine.

'This has got to be them, three occupiers like in the picture, plus servants – Mable said there would probably have been just a small number of servants – but the date is out by six years,' he said.

'Scroll down. What else does it say?' Flora asked.

'It gives the ages of the family members and the occupation of Williams Mathias. William was thirty-three, Charlotte thirty and Harriet eight in 1831 – the ages would be about right too, they could be about six years older in the drawing. William Mathias was a ship's officer, which confirms a link to the sea that Mable told us about. That's all there is. I wonder why there's nothing in the census of

1841. It's closer to the date we want but it says here that if the property isn't listed then there were no occupiers in the house at that time. No one was living in March Lane when the census of 1841 or 1851 took place,' Archie said.

'So this family were living there in 1831 but by the time the next census came along they had moved away. Have a look at 1861,' Flora said

Archie clicked to the next page, 'March Lane was unoccupied in all of those census dates. In fact according to this, the house was empty for fifty years. The next occupiers were listed in the census of 1881.'

'Were they the Mathias family?'

'No their name was Willett and there were six of them. It seems like the property changed hands then, and this is a completely different family.'

'So Mathias has to be the name of the family in the picture then,' Flora said 'and before the census of 1841 they'd left the house and didn't return. The house was occupied in 1837, which was the picture date, and then within the next four years they left and it stayed empty for nearly fifty years – that's mysterious,' Flora said.

Archie nodded. 'I agree. I think we've found our family.'

'Really? What about the letter L though? It appears in Charlotte's name and William's, though not in their surname, but it doesn't feel like that's where the clue lies,' Flora said.

'I know – and I'm not sure about the L either – but just call it my detective's intuition!' he grinned, using her words. 'Seriously though, I don't see how it could be anyone else. They are the only people listed as living in the house, apart from fifty years later. I know the dates of the census and the drawing are out by several years, but there are no other names mentioned anywhere in the database around that time.'

'I think you're right, we're right – so why did they leave March Lane?'

'They might have just moved away. If he was a sailor they could have gone to live somewhere near another port, or perhaps that's what we're supposed to find out. Maybe the letter L is a clue as to why they left,' Archie said.

'I think we should check if the Mathias family owned the property all those years?' Archie said.

'I'll go downstairs and ask Crystal to help us try and find that out,' said Flora getting up again.

Archie nodded. 'Okay – I wonder what happened to them,' he said thoughtfully.

'That, Dr Watson, is what we are going to find out!' Flora smiled, 'See if you can print the information out and we'll take it back to the incident room,' Flora said excitedly as she went in search of Crystal.

Back at Flora's house they reviewed what they'd learned.

'We need to do some more Internet research,' said Flora.

'Yes. I think we've got all that we can from the library. At least we were able to find out that March Lane remained in the Mathias name until 1880, it's just a shame that's all there was,' Archie said.

'I know, so we'll make a start with William Mathias and then see if we can find out who the two servants were,' Flora said. 'We'll also have to clean up the smashed tiles at the warehouse. If Dad goes up to the room he'll wonder what happened. It will be difficult to explain it to him now that we've already lied about the reason we went to March Lane.'

'Why don't we start everything at the weekend? I've got loads of homework this week and I really have to get it done,' Archie sighed.

'Okay, I'll write down all our questions and then we'll go to the warehouse on Saturday. Don't forget, we're going back to March Lane to help Mable with the rest of the fruit picking on Sunday. That might actually be helpful, maybe she's got some more information on her bookshelves that we can have a look at.'

CHAPTER TWENTY

Noiselessly Harriet climbed the servant's staircase up to the top floor. She heard the grandfather clock in the hallway downstairs chime one o'clock. Her mama would be so angry if she knew she was wandering around the house at this time, but she had to find out what on earth Lily had been doing charging along the corridor in the middle of the night. She crept past Mr Wickes' room – his was the largest of the attic rooms – then Cook's and when she got to Lily's bedroom door, she knocked as lightly as she could. No reply. She knocked again a little harder, conscious not to make too much noise, and then the door opened a crack.

'Lily it's me, let me in,' Harriet whispered urgently, glancing along the corridor.

'Oh... Harriet!' Lily's voice caught in her throat as she opened the door. Lily was shaking. The room was lit only by a candle in a holder on a small chest of drawers next to the bed.

'Is everything alright? Only... I saw you running along the landing and I had to see if you were well.'

'I... I... thought I was being quiet. I didn't realise you would be awake. It's so late,' Lily stammered.

'Shall we sit down?' Harriet waited for Lily to nod

before she sat on the bed. It didn't feel warm. It had obviously not been slept in.

'What on earth is the matter? Please tell me. You know just about everything about me. You can trust me,' said Harriet.

Lily sat down next to her and the springs on the old bed creaked harshly.

She sighed and seemed as though she was about to cry, 'Oh Harriet! I wouldn't know where to start.'

'What about at the beginning?' Then Harriet thought again. 'But… I don't want to *make* you tell me anything. You have to do it yourself. If you wish me to leave then I shall. I just want you to know that if something is wrong, and by the state of you it seems there is, then I might be able to help. Whatever you say will go no further, especially after all the secrets I have confided in you.' Harriet stared at Lily whose pale face and wide eyes considered her in the flickering candlelight.

'I've done something I'm not proud of, it could cost me my job but if you trust me as you say you do, then I'll tell you… and maybe two heads will be better than one.'

Lily made the decision quickly and, without thinking about the consequences, she told Harriet everything, praying that she would be true to her word.

When Lily had finished Harriet was staring at her with awe.

'You are probably the bravest, most courageous person I have ever met, next to Papa,' Harriet stated.

'You won't tell?' asked Lily.

'No! I am just shocked that you would do such a thing, risk your job and your life here, for... for us,' and she hugged Lily.

'Oh, I'm so relieved! I didn't do it for any other reason than to try and find out why the master was so worried. I wasn't snooping, even though it might look that way. Do you believe me?'

'Of course I believe you. How many times must I tell you? We are friends and that means so much to me. If I thought you had done the wrong thing I would say so, but I would certainly never go telling tales to Mama or Papa. But now I'm curious too. I wonder what this secret research is. What could he have possibly discovered that could endanger us? And then what could we do to help anyway?'

'Perhaps, now that we know, we must remain extra cautious for the next few days whilst the papers are in your papa's possession. I'm certain that once they are locked away safely then your papa and Mr Darwin will return to their normal selves again and the worrying will stop.'

'You may be right about Papa and Mr Darwin, but I think you are wrong about the research – we *have* to find it. Perhaps I should approach Papa.'

Lily felt sick. She had not expected this. 'Oh, no, no! I would certainly lose my job! He would want to know how you came about the information.'

'Yes that's a stupid idea. Alright we must find the papers ourselves, and perhaps I can say that I found them and ask what they are.'

'No, you can't do that! Your father and Mr Darwin

have devised their own plan, and I think that we should leave well alone.'

'But if we are not going to do anything then what was the purpose of risking your job? You must have really believed you could do something.'

'I did... but I think it was a mistake. It was childish and stupid to believe that a girl like me could really do anything at all.'

'No don't be silly. We just have to make the most of what we know. We don't have much time if Papa is to leave at the end of the week. In the meantime, I will search around the house when Papa is out on business. Aren't you just a little interested?'

'Yes I am – but not if it means we will get into trouble.' Lily yawned, 'I have to be up at four o'clock, Harriet, I've got to let the chimney sweep in. If you don't mind I need to go to bed or I'll never lift my head from the pillow when it's time to get up.'

Harriet stood up, 'Poor you. Will you come up to my room when you get a chance? Would it be alright after lunch? We shall decide what to do, if anything and don't worry, I shan't do a thing you don't want me to, it will be your decision in the end.'

Lily smiled, 'You are a good friend. I'll try to get away from the sweep as soon as I can.'

They hugged quickly before Harriet left.

Lily climbed into bed but she knew that sleep would evade her again. Her mind was swirling like leaves in the wind. She was glad that she had told Harriet, but she had not expected her reaction. Lily *was* curious as to the nature of Mr Darwin's secret discovery but she now knew that she would not be able to help. The sooner the master took the papers from the house, the better. She hoped that Harriet would not go searching for them. She would tell her tomorrow to leave well alone.

CHAPTER TWENTY-ONE

When Flora and Archie arrived at the warehouse on Saturday morning they found lots of people milling around. Saturday was their busiest day and Flora usually helped her dad with customers. She was always happy to show them around, or at least point them in the right direction. Her dad said it was important for people to explore the warehouse themselves because even if they came in wanting one thing, it was such a trove of treasures that they usually went out with something they had not expected to buy.

But today her mood sank. She didn't have the time to help anyone if she wanted to get up to the top floor and tidy up. She knew Archie was thinking the same. They tried to sneak past her dad but he caught them.

'Flora. Archie. There you are,' he was pleased to see them. 'This is my daughter Flora who I was telling you about,' he said turning to a plump lady with a Mary Quant bobbed hair style. She was wearing a brown shirt and yellow mini-skirt that Flora thought was much too short.

'Flora will take you upstairs to the tile room. She's been sorting the tiles up there for weeks, I'm sure she can find you a match.' He turned to Flora smiling. 'I'll need some help with customers when you come down. The old girl hasn't been this busy since great-grandfather Morris opened his doors!' Then he charged off in the direction of a man who was closely examining the roll-top baths.

Flora was horrified.

'Um... um,' she could think of no excuse as the woman waddled over to her on pointy shoes with heels so high that she appeared to be balancing on stilts.

'Oh good; this is the one I need to match, dear,' she gave Flora an ugly cream and orange tile. 'I'm into retro. It's the 1970s, dear. I want to put them on my kitchen wall. Do you think you have any like this?'

'No I don't think we have,' Archie jumped in, hoping to put the woman off. 'It's a long way up to the top floor too,' he said glancing at her feet.

'I could run a marathon in these shoes, dear. I'd like to see this room all the same. I've got some more tiles in my bag that I want to match and your father has been telling me all about the selection you have. Come on, show me the way,' she said pushing past Archie, making for the stairs.

Archie and Flora glared at each other, then Flora quickly caught up with the woman and moved in front of her, leading the way up the old staircase. What could she do? She would have to think of something when they got to the room – perhaps she'd say that they'd had an earthquake.

Flora took her time; she was trying to think of an excuse as to how a heap of broken tiles came to be strewn all over the floor.

When they got to the third floor landing she was walking so slowly that a tortoise could have overtaken her.

She knew she was beginning to annoy the customer.

'Come on dear. I don't have all day.'

'This is it... I'm sorry about the... mess...' but Flora had to stop herself from stumbling backwards. The room was neat and so tidy that she could not have done a better job. The tiles were all back in their crates and boxes. The broken floor was gone, swept away by something unknown.

'What a tidy room! I'll just go and have a rummage,' the woman remarked and proceeded further to look through the boxes and crates arranged in neat rows around the room.

Archie whispered to her, 'How did this happen?'

'I don't know!' she said with a hiss.

Archie noticed something on the rug. He walked over, picked it up and went back to Flora who was now leaning against the wall, still disturbed by the eerie tidiness.

'What is it?' she asked quietly, the woman was bending over a crate and being dangerously close to showing her underwear.

He opened his hand, 'It's a key. Did you leave it there?'

Flora's raised eyebrows said enough.

'Okay, I know you didn't leave it. Do you think our *friend* might have left it? Another clue?' Archie's asked quietly.

Flora took it from him. It was tiny, the brass tarnished to a marmite brown. The top was fashioned in an ornate scroll. It was obviously very old.

'Of course it's our next clue,' she whispered. 'Dad hasn't been up here and unless Colin has learned to stand on all fours and use a sweeping brush, then it's not him either,' she said sarcastically but then regretted it when she saw Archie's face. 'I'm sorry. It's just really unnerved me seeing the room like this. Let's get rid of madam retro and we can have a proper talk.'

She went over to the woman. 'Did you find anything?'

'No dear. Just tiles that are much too old but I haven't searched through those yet,' she said pointing at more crates against the furthest wall, then she glanced at her watch.

'Why don't I look through those for you? If you leave me your number I can ask my dad to give you a call if we find any,' said Flora.

'Would you dear? That would be great. It's far too dusty in here and my allergies will soon get started. Here's my card, my mobile is on the bottom.' She gave Flora a purple card printed with the words *'In Retrospect – the vintage way to live life'*. Flora had no idea what that meant and wasn't going to ask. She took it and put it in her pocket.

'I'll be off then, I have a nail appointment I don't want to be late for. Thanks for your help, dear,' and she wobbled out of the room.

'Bye. Thank you.' Flora called after her then sunk down on the rug in the middle of the room.

'Do we have any tiles from the 1970s?' Archie asked.

'Hundreds,' Flora said 'but if I'd told her that she would have been here all day. I'll have a dig through them later and if I find any to match that revolting tile she brought I'll get Dad to phone her.'

She opened her palm. The key was resting there offering her something but exactly what she didn't know.

'Got any ideas?' she asked Archie.

'Nope,' he replied.

'Me neither.'

'Let's go and do some more Internet research. We won't need to clean up now,' he was looking at the spotless room.

'I wonder what happened to the broken tiles,' Flora shuddered.

'I don't know and I don't care. But if your dad or Mable wants to see them then we are in deep trouble,' Archie said.

'Come on, my poor Dad seemed like he was rushed off his feet. We'll have to stay and help him for a bit.'

They stood up but Flora paused as she noticed a lump underneath the old rug she'd been sitting on. Archie spotted it at the same time.

They looked at each other. She hesitated before pulling back the rug and sending dust into the still air. Resting on the floorboards was a sooty tile.

Flora's breath caught in her throat and she felt the goosebumps rise on her arms. This time Archie was braver and he picked it up. He cleaned the tile with the bottom of his jumper and a beautiful tile emerged, the heart of a white Tudor rose.

Archie's voice cracked when he finally spoke, 'The missing tile... the one we couldn't find... What do you think it means?'

'I don't know but we have to get out of here. I have a

terrible feeling that we're being watched.'

'You're right,' he said quickly, 'come on – we need to get back downstairs! Whatever's going on here doesn't feel like a game!'

The two of them rushed from the room then they broke into a run along the dark corridor, Flora clutching the key and Archie holding tightly onto the tile.

Several hours later, having retreated to her bedroom after their fish and chip supper, and leaving her dad asleep on the sofa, they were sat in their usual place on the floor, their backs against the warm radiator.

Flora was holding the key and Archie the tile.

'I know that this is spooky but we've started now, we have to finish it,' Flora said. She'd gained her composure again.

The fear she'd felt had faded.

'You're right,' Archie said, 'but that doesn't make it any less scary. I was frightened out of my wits there today.'

'Me too, but we need to try and be rational. Whoever this ghost is, it's actually working *for* us. It wants us to find out something. It won't hurt us – at least I don't think it will,' she knew that she didn't sound very convincing.

'I was thinking the same. Why would it be leaving us clues if it wanted to harm us? It needs help, and I reckon it feels creepy because it *is* creepy. It's not natural for something that's dead to be here, in this world,' Archie said slowly.

'This key obviously opens something, and the tile *must*

have some meaning,' said Flora.

'Maybe the tile is the ghost's way of letting us know we're on the right track.'

'Yes – that must be it, a message that the link we've made with Mable's house is the right one. Well done, Dr Watson!'

'But... how do you suppose the ghost knows we've made the link?' Archie asked.

'I have no idea. Perhaps it sensed it. I know as much about ghosts as you do. We were talking about doing the Internet research on the family; it could have been listening...' said Flora.

Archie didn't like that thought at all.

Flora got the laptop from her desk then sat back down next to him. 'We need another plan,' she said.

'What about starting with the Mathias family?' Archie said.

'Okay.' She loaded Google.

'Try that ancestry site – Ancestors R Us – I've got a password.'

Flora looked at him quizzically.

'I was trying to research my family tree once,' he explained.

She raised her eyebrows.

'It was when I thought that my mum wasn't really my mum. I was hoping to maybe find my real mum out there. Stupid, I know,' Archie said sadly.

Flora felt so sorry for him.

'What's the password?' she asked kindly.

'Don't laugh. "Handsomeprince" all one word.'
Flora grinned, 'Is that what you think you are?'
'No. Now shut up and let's see what we can find.'

CHAPTER TWENTY-TWO

Harriet had escaped into the garden. Her governess had not come to the house today and so she found herself with time on her hands. She had seen Lily traipsing around behind the chimney sweep and two dirty, sooty boys and she had pulled her aside and quietly arranged to meet in her room at half past two.

Her mama and papa were out for the day and so she had taken the opportunity to squirrel herself away in the glass house. She loved the glass house, almost as much as she loved reading a book in her papa's study.

It had been over two years since she had first set foot in the glass house. Her mama's irritation had soon turned to curiosity when she realised how good Harriet was at growing things. First it was her seeds, then she used that knowledge to grow flowers and shrubs and that was soon followed by growing her first vegetables. She believed that Mama now admired what she could do in the garden, although perhaps she would never say so. She had even bought Harriet a pair of soft kid gloves for gardening. Because Harriet knew it was her mama's way of accepting what she was doing she pretended to like the gift, but she rarely wore them, she preferred to feel the soil between her fingers and under her nails.

The smell of earthy mulch and the warmth of the glass house made her smile, autumn was almost over and the atmosphere inside had a welcoming, cosy feel.

As well as a handy man around the house and second carriage man when he was needed, Joseph was also the family's gardener. He didn't live in but came from the village every day. Harriet liked Joseph. He had made the secret drawer for her and not said a word to anyone. She knew that he was trustworthy and kind and he seemed to know exactly what to do in any situation. And he was a wonderful gardener, he had 'green fingers' her papa said and she now knew exactly what that meant – Joseph could grow just about anything.

After she and Papa had planted her seeds in long trays it had been Joseph who had helped her to nurture and grow the seedlings into stronger plants. When the green shoots had pushed themselves up through the dark soil in the trays, it was Joseph's idea to plant only half of them into the garden in case they failed outside, so that they would still have half of the plants left. He was almost as excited as Harriet to see if they took to the ground after the warmth of the glass house. He had warned Harriet that the grasses were better suited to a hotter and sunnier climate than theirs, so they probably wouldn't last long, but to their great surprise that had not been the case. The plants grew well and by the end of the first summer Harriet had a small patch of waist-high grasses that had delighted her. When winter came the grasses, by then tall and willowy and the colour of golden hay, flowered unexpectedly during one night. The flowers appeared all at once; dazzling orange stars that smelled of honey.

Now that she had some time she would plant last year's seeds ready for transplanting into the garden in spring.

Joseph had left her a small crate of compost that he had dug from the outside heap for her to trowel into trays. The loamy smell of the earth stung her nose as she removed the lid. She opened the small tool chest that was underneath the planting bench to look for the trowel. She rifled through the chest but it was not there. She went to the outside shed, a small wooden container leaning against the garden wall, built to hold the larger gardening tools. The shed was always locked, so she took the key from underneath an upturned flowerpot and opened the door wide. Inside the tools were arranged neatly along the walls and on shelves around the top. The trowel was too small to be hung from a hook, so she ran her hands along the shelves, whilst standing on her tiptoes. She felt around, conscious of the spiders that lurked in their webs and had run across her hands in the past. She couldn't see but as she shuffled her hand along she felt garden twine and a pair of secateurs, an oil can, some candles and a box of matches. On the shelf at the back of the shed her fingertips touched something hard and square but even when stretching out she couldn't quite reach it.

Harriet went back into the glass house and picked up an old wooden vegetable crate, took it back into the shed, turned it upside down and stood on it. Whatever it was was wrapped in an old brown sack. Harriet tugged at it and it quickly came free but it was a bulky package and she lost her balance. As she fell to the floor the old sack landed heavily on top of her.

'Ow!' she yelped.

Harriet wasn't sure what was the most painful, her bottom, her hands or her ankle. Winded, she stayed where she was on the floor to catch her breath before tentatively standing up. To her relief her arms and legs were all working but quite sore and scraped from her fall. If Mama had seen her she would have had 'a fit and turned blue!' she thought and smiled despite the pain. She picked up the sack, carried it outside then locked the shed door.

Once inside the glass house Harriet lifted the sack onto the planting bench with a thud. Inside, as she had suspected, were four thick journals and a sheaf of a hundred or so loose papers clipped together with a small clothes peg. There was also a little glass pot of seeds which thankfully had not been broken in the fall from the shelf.

The garden shed was the safe place that her father had told Mr Darwin about, a hiding place until he took the research to the port at the end of the week, and he had *almost* been right. There wasn't much gardening going on at this time of year. They had picked the fruit from the apple and plum trees and the garden was almost dormant, pausing for winter. They were waiting for the flowering of the 'stars', as Harriet had named them, and whilst there was always a small job to do, it wasn't the busiest of months.

Joseph might have found the sack but would have been

clever enough to realise it was not his business to go nosing into it and so it probably would have stayed safely hidden for a few days, had Harriet's governess not been ill with influenza. It was actually a good hiding place Harriet thought. It was away from the house and under lock and key without it being noticeably so.

Harriet sat down on a small wooden milking stool, feeling so nervous that her hands shook.

The journals were slightly larger than her own diary but with more pages and hard, red covers, they were labelled one to four. She opened the journal labelled "CD – 1 – a private account". She found, just as the label had announced, that it was Mr Darwin's private diary. The writing was tiny and scrawling and Harriet struggled to read most of the words.

It seemed that he had written the diary on his return from his voyage on the *Beagle*. He referred to his 'field notes' which were obviously something different to the journal she was now reading. He spoke of his intrigue about the flora and fauna he had encountered on his travels and, whilst he didn't go into detail, he spoke of experiments that he might conduct now that he was home.

He had made some small drawings of lizards, which Harriet could hardly believe were real, and the 'immense' tortoises that he had encountered on his voyage, but mostly the information she could glean from his terrible handwriting was that something had made him think about… what? She could not make that out. It was so frustrating that even though she had now found what her papa and Mr Darwin had discussed in the study, she still could not make sense of what he had actually written down.

She skipped forward through the pages of undecipherable writing and found nothing of importance. She took diary number two and tried again but to her disappointment found very little that she was able to read. He mentioned some experiments at his laboratory but nothing that told her about an incredible discovery.

Feeling deflated and a little cross, she opened the third book and found that it was slightly easier to understand. He had written about a series of experiments that he had carried out. Once again Harriet flicked quickly through, now aware that time was getting on and at any moment Joseph could appear or even worse – her papa.

The experiments were undertaken on numerous plants that Mr Darwin had brought home from all over the world, though the reasons why he had carried them out was still not clear to her due to his poor handwriting. Many times he referred to other notes in his *Beagle Journals*. She turned quickly to the end of the journal and on the last few pages found the heading "Conclusions" and saw that his handwriting was much neater. She read on hastily –

Conclusions

I have concluded that this plant, in particular the seeds from this plant, have quite unbelievable healing properties. Having tested them time and again I can only deduce an almost 'magical' form of healing that takes place. As I am

112

a scientist and do not believe in magic, I must assume that the plant holds an, as yet, undiscovered medicinal property, that we in the modern world know nothing of. As my method describes in detail but I will repeat here - the seeds were ground with water and made into a paste and a teaspoon amount administered to the wound. The wound, which was made with a penknife, then healed completely within a twenty-four hour timescale. There was no visible scarring where the wound had been!

Personal observations

How can this be possible? It seems I have found a 'miracle' cure which, if used correctly, could change the face of medicine and our world completely. But I am getting away from myself. I must be careful not to use the word 'miracle' too hastily. The experiments have, so far, been carried out (secretly) on the small mice and rats in my laboratory. The next step would be to try out this poultice on larger animals before I think about human test cases - but again I am getting carried away. Before that I wish to try the possibility of healing broken bones which would involve feeding the seeds to injured animals.

Human experiments will not take place until I can be sure that there are no adverse effects on the mice and rats, which I am currently observing, then perhaps cats or dogs. Finally I am unsure of trusting anyone but my good friend WM *with this research, I fear this information, in the wrong hands, could do more damage than good.*

Harriet could hardly breathe. She had found it! Her head spun and she stood up so quickly that she felt dizzy. Mr Darwin had discovered something incredible, almost unbelievable.

No wonder he was so concerned about others finding his research, people would think he was quite mad unless he could *prove* that what he had discovered was more than "magic".

She had to read more. She put the book back into the sack and as she reached for the last journal, she glanced through the windows towards the house and saw her papa walking across the lawn waving.

'Oh no!' she muttered as she panicked and grabbed the sack, pushing it into the tool chest underneath the planting bench. Just as she had shut the lid and stood up, her papa opened the door into the glass house.

'Are you alright, Harriet?' he asked as he walked in. There was concern on his face. 'You look very flushed.' He came to her and put his hand to her head. Harriet knew she was burning not with fever but with the shame of almost getting caught.

'You are hot. How long have you been here? Too long perhaps,' he said, tutting his disapproval. 'I know this is your favourite place but you must still put time into your studies if ever you are to become a scientist.' Then he smiled gently at her. 'Come on, I've come to get you for tea and crumpets. Shopping with your mama has made me ravenous.' He took her hand and led her from the glass house. Harriet saw him glance surreptitiously at the garden shed as they passed by. Thank goodness she had locked the door.

'There, you see, your colour is changing already. Perhaps it was a little too warm inside for you,' he said and Harriet nodded, feeling both uncomfortable and excited at the same time and already thinking about what she must do tonight.

CHAPTER TWENTY-THREE

Archie's *AncestorsRUs.com* was too vague to be useful. They couldn't find anything that related to *their* Mathias family but it did eventually lead them to more interesting websites. Whilst it took them several hours of searching and surfing they finally found it – a valuable clue. Flora spotted it first.

'This says that William Mathias was an officer on the *Beagle*'s first voyage around the world.'

'Why does that sound familiar?' Archie asked.

'The *Beagle* was the ship that Charles Darwin sailed on. It was the journey that started him thinking about the origin of the species and natural selection.'

'You've lost me,' Archie said, puzzled.

'I don't know a lot about it but I think it was on that voyage around the world that he began to develop his theories about evolution; how different species of animals adapt and evolve to their natural habitat. Hold on...' Flora typed into her laptop. 'It says here that he published his *Journal and Remarks* in 1839, about his voyage on the HMS *Beagle*, but he didn't actually publish his book *On the Origin of Species* until twenty years later.'

'Oh yes I remember that. The tree of life. We did something on that in science and I think there was a David

Attenborough programme on the TV about him,' said Archie.

'His book caused controversy in Victorian times. People thought he was going against the Church.'

'So William Mathias was on that journey too. That's amazing! What date did it set sail?' asked Archie.

'1831. The expedition was supposed to be two years but instead it lasted almost five. It returned in 1836.'

'That's a year before the drawing was made.'

'Did William go on any more journeys after that one?'

'Darwin did, much later but it doesn't say anything more about William Mathias. That's the only thing I can find. After that date there's nothing about him at all. It's like he disappeared,' Flora said.

'Or perhaps he just didn't do anything that was notable. I mean, to be on that ship, that's quite amazing. He might even have been a celebrity.'

'That's more likely to have been the Captain rather than an officer. It says the Captain's name here, there are a lot of web pages about his life,' Flora said still clicking on her laptop.

'What about Charlotte Mathias?' Archie asked.

'Nothing – and I can't find Harriet either.'

'Well it seems to me that the most important date is 1837. That's the date on the drawing and that's the last we can trace any of the family. There's no family tree, and the only thing we know is that William Mathias sailed on the *Beagle* from 1831 to 1836.'

'We have the tile and the key and the letter L don't

forget,' Flora sighed 'but it doesn't seem much and although we know where the floor came from I still don't feel any closer than I did when we began. Being a detective is harder than I imagined it would be.'

'I know it is but you're forgetting two things,' said Archie.

'What?'

'One. We can have a look in Mable's library again or perhaps she has something else up in her attic rooms on the Mathias family. Now that we know their names it might sound familiar to her. And two, we also have a –,' he hesitated for a moment, '– a ghost. We could ask it what it really wants.'

Flora was shocked. 'I hope you're not serious about option number two,' but she'd seen the look on Archie's face. 'You mean you'd go back and try to speak to it?'

'We could go together,' he suggested, although Flora could hear his uncertainty.

'I don't know, Archie. I'm sure it's trying to tell us something but to actually go and look for it... I think that would be too dangerous,' said Flora seriously.

'Yeah, maybe you're right. It's just so frustrating not knowing,' Archie sighed, but Flora could see his relief.

'Let's finish now,' said Flora changing the subject. 'We'll take what we found in the library and this bit of information to Mable's tomorrow and see if she can help us. She seems nice enough.'

'I still don't want to tell her about the ghost,' said Archie.

'I know, but we might have to eventually, especially if

she can help us. Let's just see if she can give us anything else. I promise I won't say a word unless we both agree.'

Archie smiled, 'Okay. What do you want to do now?'

'How about vegging out and watching a DVD by the fire? We could watch *The Goonies* for the two hundredth time.'

'Great idea,' Archie jumped up and grabbed Flora's arm. She only just managed to catch her laptop as he pulled her up onto her feet.

'I'll get the DVD,' he said, 'you light the fire.'

CHAPTER TWENTY-FOUR

Harriet wasn't able to meet Lily, she had to have tea and crumpets with her mama and papa. Although she tried to seem interested in her mama's purchases and her papa's preparations for his next voyage, her mind drifted away as to how she was going to obtain the last journal. Lily, too, was so busy after spending the morning trailing behind the chimney sweep and his rabble of boys, that she could not escape from her duties for long enough to even say hello.

Once she had been excused, Harriet raced up to her room and sat on her bed. She only had two days left before Papa took the journals to the port, and he might retrieve them from the garden shed at any point before then. She was also concerned that, if he should go and look for them, they would not be where they were supposed to be. She hoped that he would be too busy to do so.

Harriet needed to retrieve the final journal quickly, and she would have to do it tonight. If she could, she would try to get Lily to come with her as she didn't like the idea of going outside in the garden alone when it was dark. Even though it was quite safe and had a high brick wall, it was something she had never done before and although she wasn't afraid of the dark, it made her feel a little jittery.

*

Time dragged for the rest of the day as Harriet waited for daylight to disappear. She wasn't able to speak with Lily at all because she was still too busy, so she decided that there would be lots more to tell her if she went without her. She would be brave and go to the glass house alone.

Once dinner had been eaten, it was, at last, time for bed. Her mama came up to her room to brush out her hair and plait it for her. Harriet put on her long warm nightdress and got into bed. The fire in the grate was dying but the room was still warm.

'Don't stay up and read too late Harriet or you will have dark circles under your eyes that you will not be able to rid yourself of,' her mama warned.

'I won't, Mama. I promise,' Harriet smiled her most angelic smile and hoped that her mother would not see through it.

'Alright. Goodnight. Say your prayers before you blow out your lamp.'

'Yes, Mama, I will.'

Her mama closed the bedroom door behind her and Harriet laid her head back on the pillow and waited. She read for a time but her eyes floated across the words on the page and she did not take in any of the story. She listened as the household settled. Her mind was active and alert to every noise from downstairs. She heard Mr Wickes lock and bolt the front door, then heard him say goodnight to her father.

Finally her papa was walking along the landing. Harriet

quickly closed her eyes and pretended to be asleep, still holding her book. He opened the door quietly as he came into her room. Taking the book from her hand he lightly kissed her forehead and then blew out her lamp before he left.

Harriet sighed. She waited until the clock chimed twice downstairs before she pulled back the bedcovers and slipped out. She took her boots from under her bed and tugged them silently onto her stockingless feet. Taking a cardigan that lay in a crumpled heap on her bedroom chair, she buttoned it up over her nightdress. From her dressing table she took a candle and some matches and put them into her cardigan pocket then she tiptoed to the bedroom door. Harriet opened it a tiny crack and listened. It was quiet and dark. The only sound she heard was the ticking grandfather clock. Silently and holding her breath she crept to the servants' staircase, opening the door she made her way carefully down each step and into the empty kitchen.

She knew that the key was kept on the shelf above the back door, she had seen Mr Wickes put it there once or twice. She reached up onto her toes, felt along the shelf and finding the heavy brass key she unlocked the door.

The cold air smacked at her face as soon as it was open; her cardigan was little defence against the bitterness of the wind. Harriet closed the door quietly behind her but made sure not to lock it before climbing the stone staircase warily, worried that she might trip over her nightdress and fall on the hard stone steps.

There was no moonlight and the garden lay before her,

a vast expanse of black. It was so dark she could make out only shadows as her eyes slowly adjusted. The wind rustled and blew the trees and shrubs and she suddenly felt quite scared, but she knew the way to the glass house well and so she cautiously continued in that direction.

Harriet stumbled forward and eventually reached her destination. As she stepped inside, the warmth comforted her. Harriet lit the candle and stood it on the floor.

She went quickly to the tool chest under the planting table and lifted the lid. To her dismay she saw that the sack was gone!

Her knees buckled. Tears came as she realised the gravity of the situation. What was she to do! Where was the sack? She considered for a moment, perhaps it was back in the garden shed? She took the candle and went outside. She found the key under the pot, opened the door and rushed inside. The crate she'd used earlier was leant against the wall and she used it to stand on again. Harriet almost cried out with relief when she felt the sack on the shelf, back in its original place! She pulled it free, with more care this time.

It must have been Joseph. If it had been her papa she would certainly have known about it. He had found the sack in the tool chest and returned it. He was so honest. Just as he had fitted her secret drawer without asking any questions, she was sure Joseph wouldn't have read the journals, he would simply have returned them knowing that it wasn't his business. Harriet thought that she might just love Joseph for considering her so! She would explain everything to him when he came on Friday and tell him how grateful she was.

Now she acted quickly. Rummaging in the sack for the fourth journal, she removed it and with difficulty, hoisted the sack back up onto the shelf. She quickly locked the shed door, returned the key and rushed across the garden, tripping over her nightdress several times.

Her teeth were chattering, the wind cutting through her as she raced down the steps to find the kitchen door… open wide.

Harriet felt like she had been punched and thought that she was going to be sick. She was certain that she had shut the door. She hesitated on the threshold. The kitchen was in darkness just as she had left it. It took all of her courage and her legs wobbled as she stepped inside.

The kitchen was so warm compared with outside that the sudden change in temperature made her shudder involuntarily. Her eyes were already adjusted to the dark as she looked around the room. She found nothing out of the ordinary. Her heart hammered against her ribs and she put her hand to her chest, as if by touching it she could stop it thundering.

She had yet to move, for she feared that there may be someone hiding in the shadows. Then she bravely took another step forward and stood still again. If someone was inside she knew that she could scream loud enough to wake the entire house.

She waited until she finally realised, with slow relief, that there was no one there. She closed the door, paused to try and stop her hands shaking, then turned the key and locked out the night. She tried to quiet her anxiety; perhaps she had not closed the door sufficiently for the latch to catch, she had been rushing – but it had terrified her to see the kitchen door standing open.

Exhaustion suddenly overcame her and all she now wanted was to get to bed as quickly as she could. She did not know how long she had been outside but Mr Wickes was an early riser and she did not want to get caught. She would read the journal in the morning and it would not be difficult to slip to the shed to replace it before her father took the others to the port.

When Harriet was at last safely back inside her bedroom she reached into the bottom of her wardrobe, found the little brass key hidden in an old shoe at the very back and turned the lock. She placed the journal in the secret compartment on top of her own diary; it was a tight fit. She closed it, silently thanking Joseph once again and then scrambled into bed.

CHAPTER TWENTY-FIVE

The last of the apples and plums had been gathered and Flora, Archie, her dad and Mable were sat in front of a glowing fire in the study. The sweet smell of ripe fruit still lingered around each of them. They had worked for several hours and as payment for their help, Mable had cooked them a Sunday lunch, complete with a plum and apple cinnamon crumble smothered with fresh vanilla custard. Flora had never been so full and her dad was rubbing his stomach with happy satisfaction.

It felt to Flora as though they'd known Mable much longer than just two weeks. She was open, kind and laughed a lot, and was a very different person to the abrupt woman that they had first met at her garden gate. She chuckled at the stories her dad told about some of his more eccentric customers and the tales about Colin the dog, whose name she loved and whom she said must be brought along next time they came. It was obvious to Flora that Mable missed having people around her. Flora got the sense that although Mable was used to being alone, she would prefer not to be.

'That was a delicious meal, Mable. Where did you learn to cook like that?' asked her dad.

'I've travelled a lot, Horace. I spent much of my youth

in Canada and learned to cook there.'

'Where did you live in Canada?' Flora was interested in hearing Mable's story as she'd given very little away about her life until now.

'I moved around but for a time I lived in Vancouver, first in the city and then I lived on Vancouver Island for several years. Later, I went east and spent some time in Kitchener, a small town outside Toronto.'

'You still have a little bit of your accent,' said Flora, finally understanding where it came from.

'Are you married, Mable?' asked Archie. Flora hoped he didn't sound too nosy.

Fortunately Mable smiled at him 'I was... but my husband died.'

'Oh, I'm sorry, that's awful' Archie said, 'he must have been very young.'

'Yes, he was,' Mable said sadly, with such a forlorn look that Flora quickly changed the subject. 'Do you want to know what we've found out about the house?'

'Of course,' Mable said her expression changing to a smile again.

Flora retrieved her rucksack from the floor and pulled out her files and the new floor tile, which she passed to Mable.

'Well, this is most definitely part of the floor that is drawn in the picture. It looks like it could be the centre tile.' She was peering closely at it. 'And you *are* organised!' Mable said admiring Flora's neat notes.

'Takes after her dad,' her dad said. Flora could see that

his eyes had taken on their usual sleepy after-dinner look.

'I think my dad's going to fall asleep,' said Flora feeling slightly embarrassed.

'After a delicious Sunday roast like that it would only be polite for me to have forty winks,' he said.

'You're right, Horace, it wouldn't be Sunday without a nap after lunch,' said Mable happily.

Within minutes Flora's dad was sleeping quietly in the big armchair next to the fire.

'Sorry,' she said.

'Don't apologise, it's nice for this house to feel like a home again, full of people, even sleepy people, as it should be.'

'It's so comfortable here and it's like we've known you for ages,' said Flora.

'I was thinking the same. It's wonderful to have your company and I'm glad your dad feels at home here too,' said Mable, glancing at her snoozing father.

'Do you have any family around here, Mable? You said you grew up in this area,' asked Archie.

'No I don't, not any more, my family have all passed away. I'm sorry to say that it's just me left.'

'But you don't look old enough to be the last!' Archie exclaimed.

'Good genes,' said Mable.

Archie laughed. 'I have the feeling that I've put my foot in it at least twice today,' he said as he blushed strawberry red.

'Don't be silly, you've done nothing of the sort. It's

refreshing to have some honest young people around. Now that's enough about me, let me hear what you've found out about my house.'

'Well it isn't a huge amount, but we think we know the name of the family in the drawing,' Flora flicked through her file and found the photocopy of the picture Mable had made for her.

'We think that this is William, Charlotte and Harriet Mathias; they were the first owners. We traced William Mathias and found that he was an officer on the HMS *Beagle*, the ship that took Charles Darwin on his first voyage around the world. We weren't so lucky though finding anything about Charlotte or Harriet Mathias.'

Mable seemed thoughtful for a moment, as if she was remembering something.

'That name is familiar.'

'Really? Do you think you might have some information on them here?' Archie asked, looking up at the bookshelves that lined the room.

'I don't know... but I will have a look later. Was there anything else?'

'Only what we found in the 1831 census. By the time the next census came around in 1841 there was no sign of them. In fact, nobody lived here for nearly fifty years after. This is the last we can find of the Mathias family, this date and picture. After 1837 they seem to have disappeared.'

'Or died,' Archie said, 'it's really strange that the house was empty for so long and yet it still belonged to the Mathias family until it changed owners in the 1880s.'

Mable sighed, 'What a terrible shame. I thought perhaps you'd found out what had happened to them.'

'You almost sound as if you know them,' Flora smiled.

'Do I? No, no... I just meant it would have been nice to know more about the first people that lived here. At least you discovered that.'

'Oh,' Flora said, but she had a strange feeling that Mable was keeping something from them.

'I think we've come to a dead end,' Archie sighed.

'Don't sound so disappointed, Archie. After all, you still have some history about the house and it was the tile floor that got you interested in the first place. You might not know much about the Mathias family but you have a lot of information about who lived here after them. That was the purpose of your project, wasn't it?' asked Mable. She was staring at them.

Flora and Archie looked at each other, they were deciding what to tell Mable. Should they take a chance and reveal the true reason for their curiosity? Did they know her well enough to think she would believe them? They were both waiting for the other to speak. Flora waited longer; she didn't want to do anything that would upset Archie.

'Well, it's a little more complicated than that,' Archie finally said quietly, looking over at Flora's dad who was still snoring lightly. 'If we tell you, you have to understand that everything we say is completely true and you must promise not to tell anyone.'

'Why don't you try me?' Mable said seriously. 'You would be surprised what I know to be true.'

So Archie began their story.

He spoke just above a whisper, so that Mable had to lean forward to hear him. Flora wasn't sure if Archie was trying not to wake her dad or if he was still uncertain about Mable's reaction.

Archie had surprised himself. He'd only met Mable twice, but there was something about her that made him think that he could tell her anything without her judging him. He stopped now and again to let Flora add details and together they told her everything.

'The latest clues were a small brass key and that tile,' said Flora pointing to the tile that Mable was still holding in her hand.

'We know that the floor came from this house, but we haven't got anywhere nearer to what the letter L stands for or what the key opens. And that's everything. Apart from what we found out about the Mathias family from the Internet, we've reached a very high brick wall,' Archie finally ended.

Mable, who had said nothing throughout their account, was very still, her face unreadable.

Then she did something that neither of them had expected.

She began to cry.

CHAPTER TWENTY-SIX

It was the smell of smoke that woke Harriet, as swiftly as smelling salts would have done had she fainted. She sat up quickly and coughed deeply. Throwing back the bed covers she went to the window. She opened the curtains which revealed the sombre, grey light of early morning. She felt dizzy and light-headed. Was she dreaming? But she realised with horror that her bedroom was filling with smoke, crawling like menacing wispy fingers underneath the door, she knew that she was awake and in terrible danger.

She raced into the hallway, knowing that she had to reach her papa and mama but the smoke was thicker in the corridor. A coughing fit seized her and she doubled over. Eyes streaming, she ran along the corridor trying desperately to call out but was unable to do so as her breath was caught again by another coughing spasm. Her throat felt as though it was lined with stinging nettles and her voice was nothing more than a croaky whisper.

Harriet began to cry hysterically. Throwing propriety to the wind she rushed into her parents' bedroom. They were still asleep and the smoke was much worse in their room.

'Papa! Mama!' she cried, but they did not move. She threw herself at her papa's side.

'Papa!' She shook him hard, but still he did not stir. An overwhelming fear gripped her as she continued to shake him over and over, 'Papa! Please, Papa! Wake up! Please!' Without thinking she slapped his face as hard as she could. At last he moved, mechanically and slowly he opened his eyes.

'Harriet?' his voice sounded heavy and hoarse.

The smoke swirled around them and she grabbed the bed sheet to cover her mouth as she pulled at his arm.

'Papa! We must go, hurry, wake Mama... please!' she cried through the material.

Her Papa began to cough too, then suddenly becoming aware of his smoky surroundings, he sat up then leapt from the bed.

'Charlotte!' He ran around to her mama's side of the bed and shook her but she did not move.

'Harriet! Hurry, rip up the bedsheet and keep your mouth covered. We must have been overcome. *Charlotte*! I will carry your mother downstairs. Quickly! We have to get out of the house now!'

Harriet tore at the sheet and held it to her mouth. As she rushed across the room, she turned and saw her papa carrying her mama who lay like a limp ragdoll in his arms. Harriet hurried along the corridor to the stairs where she stopped. At the foot of the staircase she could see flames beginning to jump at the bottom of the study door.

She was so terrified by the thought of having to go down towards the fire that she stood frozen on the top step. Her papa came rushing up behind her holding her mama.

'It's contained in my study for now, but we must hurry. The door is about to burn and then it will spread. Go!' he roared so loudly that Harriet's trance was broken and she sprinted down the stairs.

The temperature was so fierce at the bottom of the staircase it was almost unbearable. Harriet could feel the perspiration running down her back. As she reached the front door there was an explosion that shook the house and she screamed. She turned to see scorching flames coming from the kitchen stairs. She dropped the sheet from her mouth and fumbled with the lock.

Harriet pulled frantically at the door until she finally fell out into the bitterly cold morning. She gulped in mouthfuls of fresh clean air and coughed until she was sick. She heard her papa saying her mama's name over and over.

She crawled to them and asked fearfully, 'Is she alright, Papa?'

'She's breathing but I cannot get a reaction from her,' his face was distorted. 'I have to go back into the house. I must get the others. Wickes, Cook and Lily are still inside,' he said urgently.

The realisation dawned on Harriet. Lily was still in there!

'Stay with Mama. Keep talking to her,' her papa coughed violently and before she could stop him he rushed back through the front door.

Harriet held her mama's head in her lap; her dark hair was spread across her night dress like an open black fan. Her vision was blurred by her tears.

'Mama, please wake up,' she said quietly. 'Mama you must wake. I promise I will never argue with you again or be rude or insolent. Just wake up... please... *please*...' She was sobbing now and her heart, which was still pounding, felt like it was going to break.

Her despair deepened as flames burst from the broken window of her papa's study. Thick charcoal smoke billowed from the front door and she thought she would pass out from the dread she was feeling. She stared at the doorway, desperate to see her papa and feeling like a hopeless child.

Then Joseph was sitting beside her, she had not seen or heard him arrive. Harriet could hardly speak but she knew that he would know what to do.

'The smoke. I think she breathed in too much... she won't wake up...' she said desperately.

Joseph put his hand on her arm, 'Don't worry, Harri, help is coming from the village.' He looked at her mama lying motionless on the grass. 'The doctor will be here any minute. She'll be alright.' He gave her a reassuring smile. 'Where's your father?'

'Oh Joseph! Papa is inside. He went back in to get Cook and Lily and Mr Wickes.'

'Lily,' Joseph said her name, then he stood up quickly and made for the front door. Harriet grabbed at the leg of his trousers. 'No don't!' she screamed 'Not you too! Stay here. Please don't go inside!'

Joseph hesitated before he sat back beside her and before they could speak again they were surrounded by

135

men from the village. Some of the faces she recognised and some she did not, but they all regarded her with sad kindness. The men carried buckets of water and were shouting and calling to each other.

Her mama was seen by the village doctor and was carried away to a carriage.

'It's alright now, Harriet. We'll take her to the hospital and look after her. You must come as well, you have breathed in a lot of smoke too,' Doctor Daley said kindly.

But Harriet refused. She was not going anywhere until her papa returned.

'At least come away from the house,' the doctor said, resigned that he could not get her to go with him. Harriet reluctantly agreed and walked to the fence but continued to stare at the front door. Then she was lost in the crowd of men who got on with the business of putting out the fire.

It was taking too long.

The fire was fierce and the heat was breaking windows throughout the house. The men had made a winding line from the village pond, down the lane to her home, passing pails of water hand over hand to each other.

She felt as though she was splintering into tiny pieces as she started to consider that her papa might not emerge from the house again, that she would never see Lily, Cook or Mr Wickes alive. Her legs felt weak as she began to tremble.

As her last hope dissolved, her papa came charging through the front door carrying Lily in his arms.

Harriet was rooted to the ground. Her papa's nightclothes were blackened and singed but he was alive.

She could not move, all she could do was stand and stare.

She saw Mr Wickes helping Cook out into the morning air and just as she had done they both bent over and coughed until they were sick.

But Harriet could see that something was terribly wrong. Lily was not moving. Her nightdress was torn and scorched and her bare legs were visible. What Harriet saw frightened her beyond anything that she had seen before.

Lily was burned.

Her legs and arms were dark pink and raw like the skin of a pig, and it was blistering into large yellow pustules. Lily's head lolled backwards and Harriet drew in a sharp breath as she saw that her scalp was visible where her hair had been burned away. Joseph was pushing forward through the crowd gathering around them and Harriet watched as he took Lily from her papa and fell to the ground with her. Harriet finally walked unsteadily towards her papa, they hugged one another and he looked down at her sadly. She fought the urge to cry out in joy that her father was alive, but instead said a silent prayer of thanks to God.

She realised that Joseph had stepped away from Lily to allow the doctor to see to her.

Harriet suddenly knew what she had to do.

She left her papa who began talking to the men around him, his business now was to take charge. 'It's gone up the back staircase, that's why I couldn't get down that way. Lily was trapped on the landing –'

Harriet grabbed Joseph's hand. He was pale and

stunned.

'Joe!' she shouted at him '…listen to me. We can help Lily. But I need you to come with me. Now!'

'What? What do you mean?'

'Come on,' she pulled at his arm and he allowed himself to be led. Harriet dragged him around the side of the house as they passed men carrying buckets of water and sand.

'The sack, I need you to get the sack from the garden shed.'

Joseph stopped.

'I know you saw it. You put it away yesterday. I haven't got time to explain but I need what's inside it. We must get it now!'

'Harri, what… what are you talking about…?'

'I will explain later, but I'm certain it can help Lily!'

Her words were the catalyst that made Joseph move. He took Harriet's hand and they ran across the garden. They found the key under the pot and opened the shed. Joseph reached the sack easily and pulled it from the shelf. He threw it over his shoulder and without closing the door he carried it back across the garden as Harriet ran behind him.

'Wait!' Harriet cried. 'We have to leave the sack here, we can't take the books. Let me look!'

Joe passed it to her and she delved in and found the tiny glass pot.

'Leave it behind that shrub.' She pointed to a large bush and Joseph did as she asked.

'I don't know if this will work but we can at least try,' she said as they both ran back to the front of the house.

Lily was still lying on the grass. Someone had placed a blanket over her and there were people standing talking, making decisions about what to do as they waited for a carriage to come.

There was too much going on for anyone to notice as Harriet and Joseph sat themselves on the ground next to her. Lily's breathing was shallow and coming in short gasps. Her eyes were closed and her face was painfully blistered and terribly burnt. Harriet could smell what was left of her scorched hair and her skin was so badly damaged that it made her stomach churn – but she moved closer. She gently opened Lily's mouth then tipped the contents from the pot onto her tongue.

Harriet said quietly into her ear, 'I don't know if you can hear me Lily but try and swallow, it will help with the pain.'

Lily's mouth closed and all Harriet could do was hope that she had done the right thing. Joseph was crying, his tears leaving tracks on his sooty cheeks and she bit her lip willing herself not to cry too.

Someone noticed her and she was suddenly being lifted into the air, out of the way. Then Lily was carried swiftly to a waiting carriage with Joseph quickly following.

CHAPTER TWENTY-SEVEN

Flora was stunned and Archie's face said the same. They watched as Mable continued to cry.

'Mable? What's wrong?' Flora asked and she couldn't quite believe what she was seeing.

Mable shook her head, then she stood up and quickly left the room.

Flora looked at Archie.

'What on earth...?' Archie was equally as shocked by Mable's reaction.

'Did we say anything that might have offended her?' Flora asked him in a whisper.

'No, nothing. We more or less told her a ghost story, that's it. I don't understand.'

'Oh dear,' Flora was dismayed.

They had made a terrible mistake. They'd been deceived by their affection for Mable but obviously didn't know her as well as they thought they did. Flora's dad began to stir in the chair and he opened his eyes. Flora and Archie were sat like stone pillars on the sofa opposite him.

'Mmm, that was a nice nap. Have I been asleep long?' he asked.

'No, not too long, Dad,' Flora said, she was worrying about Mable.

He checked the clock on the mantle.

'It's half past six, I think we'd better get going, it's a bit of a journey home. Where's Mable?'

'Here I am, Horace,' Mable came back into the room, her voice as bright as it had been before and her face washed clean, but Flora could see that her expression was falsely bright.

Mable said to Flora and Archie, 'I've made you a plum pie to take home. It's in the bag by the front door. My telephone number is in there in case you need to phone me. I think I gave it to you last time you came but just in case.' She was staring so directly at Flora that she knew exactly what Mable was trying to tell her.

'Yes, I still have a few questions about the house,' Flora said for her dad's benefit as she watched him get up from the chair.

'Well that was a lovely day. Thank you for everything,' said her dad as he went out to the hallway to retrieve his coat.

Mable whispered to them as soon as he left the room. 'Ring me as soon as you can. I have so much I need to tell you. It is extremely important, Flora,' she said catching hold of Flora's hand and squeezing it. Her dad came back into the room

'No, thank you, you have all been a great help. You must come again, I feel we have all become great friends already.'

'Why don't you come to us next time then?' her dad said, 'Perhaps I can cook something for you.'

'That would be lovely, I shall look forward to it.'

And with that they left Mable standing at her door in the darkness of the November evening wondering what on earth had happened to make her cry.

When they eventually got back to Flora's house they were still stunned.

'I just don't understand it. I've been racking my brains wondering if we said something awful that set her off but I'm certain we didn't,' said Archie completely puzzled.

'I've been doing the same all the way home. We didn't. But when we were talking about the Mathias family I had a really strange feeling that she knew something,' Flora said.

'Really?'

Flora nodded.

'What do you think we should do now?' Archie asked.

'I'll phone her tomorrow. She made it pretty clear she wanted to speak to me.'

'This whole thing just gets creepier and creepier,' said Archie with a shudder and Flora nodded in complete agreement.

Flora and Archie had no time to discuss the events at Mable's house. They were both too busy with school work. The whole week had passed before they eventually caught up with each other.

'Did you ring her?' Archie asked flinging himself down on Flora's bed.

'I tried but I got her answer phone every time.'

'What do you think we should do?' Archie asked.

'I'll try her again now if you like.'

'Yeah, go on then.'

Flora took her mobile from her pocket and dialled Mable's number which she'd stored. The phone rang twice and suddenly Mable's voice was on the line.

'Hello, hello... who is this?' Mable sounded disorientated.

'Mable it's me Flora. I've been trying to reach you all week. Are you alright?'

'Oh, Flora, I'm so glad you phoned,' Mable's voice went away from the phone for a moment then came back, 'Can I phone you back on the landline? I can't abide these mobile devices.'

'Yes I'll be here,' Flora said and hung up.

'Old people and mobiles!' Archie said and he rolled his eyes as Flora's phone rang.

'Hello?'

'Flora it's me, Mable. That's better. I much prefer to use my home phone. Right where was I – oh yes. I've been away for the week and forgot to take my phone. I'm so sorry, that's why you couldn't get hold of me.'

'It's just that I was really worried. You asked me to call you immediately and when you didn't answer –'

'I know. I'm sorry but I had a lot of thinking to do,' Mable's voice was quiet and strained.

'You were so upset when we left you last week. Archie and I have been trying to work out what we said.'

'That's why I've been away Flora. I needed time to

think about what it is I should tell you. If it's alright with you I would like to come and see you.'

'Of course you can,' Flora was surprised by the request, 'I'll have to let dad know you're coming though, he'll want to make dinner or something.'

'No, no Flora. I take it from our last conversation that your dad knows nothing about what happened to you and Archie at the warehouse.'

'No he doesn't, not yet. Well, he knows about us uncovering the tile floor.'

'Then if it's alright with you I would like to leave it like that, for now at least.'

Flora could hear the tension in Mable's voice. 'Could you meet me at your father's warehouse? Without him knowing?'

'Umm… Yes, I suppose we could. It would have to be after he closes. I could say that Archie and I are going to the library for evening revision. It's open until nine on a Thursday,' Flora was starting to feel uncomfortable and Archie's face was asking a hundred questions.

'Shall I come on Thursday then?'

'Yes alright,' Flora said already feeling anxious.

'I will meet you there at seven. That's not too late is it?'

'No that's fine, but why don't you want to come to my house? And –'

Mable interrupted her. 'It has to be at the warehouse, or your father would know I was visiting. I can't explain now but I will tell you more when I see you.'

'Okay.' She gave Mable the address of the warehouse

and then they said their goodbyes and hung up.

'Well that wasn't at all weird,' Flora said sarcastically as she relayed the conversation to Archie.

'Perhaps we shouldn't go,' Archie said cautiously. 'I know we really like her, and I know we thought we could trust her enough to tell her about the haunting but why does she want to meet us at the warehouse? It's too freaky.'

'I agree. Part of me says we shouldn't go, but a little bit of me really wants to know what this is all about. Aren't you curious?'

'I am, I suppose, but I don't have a death wish. What if our intuition is completely wrong and she's some sort of mad axe murderer,' he said seriously.

'We'll take precautions. I'll take my phone and if something feels off, we'll call my dad and tell him everything, even the haunting bit.'

'Okay. But by the time he gets to the warehouse we could be dead and chopped up into tiny pieces,' Archie said grimly.

'But you're forgetting our secret weapon,' Flora said and Archie frowned.

'Colin!' she said triumphantly.

CHAPTER TWENTY-EIGHT

Mama is dead. She could not quite understand those words. She heard them over and over inside her head. Mama is dead. Mama is dead. Mama is dead.

Harriet was sat on a chair in Mr Darwin's small room whilst his cousin, Emma Wedgewood, who had visited them often, poured tea. She was aware of the noise of the china as the cups clinked lightly against the saucers.

'Would you like sugar, my dear?' Miss Wedgewood asked kindly.

Harriet nodded unable to let any words come from her mouth. If they did she feared that she would make too real what was being said in her head. Mama is dead.

She took the tea cup but it shook so violently in her hand that Miss Wedgewood took it back from her.

'Perhaps you should have the cup without the saucer.' She gave her the cup on its own. Harriet could only nod her thank you.

When the fire had finally been brought under control and the last embers had been drowned away, her father had gone to survey the house. He would not allow Harriet, who had sat with a kind lady from the village for the entire time, to go inside. She could clearly see that the fire had caused too much destruction for them to stay. Their only fortune lay in the fact that it had not burned to the ground. All the walls still stood and the roof remained, though the pretty red brick was invisible through the soot.

Inside was a different picture. Most of the rooms were destroyed along with the furniture and their possessions, though some of the upstairs bedrooms were still intact. The kitchen and the back staircase were gone. There was nothing left. It had all burnt away. Her papa's study, his beautiful oak desk, the spicy red Persian rug, and his entire book collection were no more. The main staircase was still standing, but only just and the staircase that Mr Wickes and Lily used, that led from the hallway down to the kitchen, was a mound of ash.

As the weary villagers left, her papa thanked them with such sincerity that Harriet had wanted to cry. Harriet and her papa were taken by carriage to Mr Darwin's lodgings, where his housekeeper, Mrs Finch, had kindly allowed them to stay. They were both still in their nightwear, dirty and dishevelled. Mrs Finch had driven out to purchase them clean clothes. Both Harriet and her papa had refused to be seen by a doctor until they had visited her mama, so they washed and changed and then they took a carriage directly to the hospital.

Harriet and her papa had visited Lily on the ground floor of the hospital first, but despite Harriet's hope, Lily was still as badly burned as she had been when her papa had carried her from the house. She was wrapped in soft bandages that wound around her head, legs and arms. Her poor face had been covered and Harriet felt a terrible overwhelming sickness. The seeds had not worked. She had been wrong. Mr Darwin's third journal had said that he had made a poultice when he had conducted his experiments but Harriet had not had the time to do so. If she had managed to read the last journal perhaps she would have known more, but the last journal was gone. She had put it in her secret compartment and the fire had taken it too. Lily was still unconscious and the nurse had whispered to her papa that she was very, very poorly.

They stayed only for a brief moment before hurrying to her mama's room on the first floor.

'May I see you for a moment, William?' Doctor Daley had said quietly, taking her papa to one side.

'Yes of course. Wait here, Harriet. We will see Mama in a few minutes.'

But Papa had been wrong.

Her mother had died just a few minutes before, when they had been visiting Lily. Mama had taken in too much smoke, her breathing had faltered and her heart had stopped.

Harriet had held her father's hand and hugged him tightly as his shoulders shuddered, yet she did not shed a tear and it made her feel so terribly guilty. She could not remember how she had walked away from the hospital, leaving her mama behind. She was so distressed, yet still she did not cry. The pain and grief that she could not express seemed to be wrapped tightly inside her like a present on her birthday, waiting to be opened but she could not even begin to tear at the paper for fear that she would collapse and die like her poor, poor mama.

At the funeral she stood solemnly at her papa's side. People she did not know came to her and shook her hand and gave her their condolences and even then she did not cry.

Thanks to Mrs Finch's compassion, Harriet and her papa had been staying at Mr Darwin's lodging house for three weeks. And in that time, there had been no tears. She could hardly bring herself to speak.

She had not returned to March Lane. Her papa had not asked her to but she knew that she could not go there even if he had. She understood that they were concerned for her. She had heard her papa speaking to Miss Wedgwood just an hour previously when she had stood outside the parlour door.

'Perhaps she should see a doctor, William,' Miss Wedgwood had said.

Her papa had replied sadly, 'No, Emma. She just cannot express herself yet. She does not realise how much like her mother she is,' then his voice cracked, 'Charlotte was the same. She contained her emotions but eventually Harriet's will come. We just have to be patient and protect her.'

'Have you told her of your plans yet?' Miss Wedgewood had asked.

'No. I will tell her once everything has been settled. I will hear from the merchant shipping company in the morning.'

'Do you think you are doing the right thing?'

'All I know is that I cannot stay, Emma. To see our home as it is, that is enough to break my heart but I could get over that – but knowing that Charlotte will never return with us, I just could not bear to live there without her. I know that Harriet feels the same.'

'Yes of course. I do understand but Charles and I worry so about you both, and in many ways he does feel responsible for this awful tragedy – and it is such a long way for you to go.'

Harriet had walked into the parlour then and the subject had been changed, she guessed what her father had been planning and when he told her she was not surprised.

They were leaving. Forever.

Her papa had booked them a passage to New Zealand, a country he had visited when journeying on the *Beagle*, a place, he had told her that was a lot like England. New Zealand would be their new home.

Harriet was numb. The emotions she was battling with were still tightly locked away. She did not wish to return to March Lane, about that her father had been right. She couldn't bear to live in a house without her mama: playing the piano, walking in the garden, coming to her room at night to brush out her hair. It was too devastating to contemplate and she was grateful to her papa for making the decision.

Mama was dead and Lily had not recovered. It had been four weeks and her papa had told her that Lily was still

150

gravely ill, hovering between life and death. Her papa wanted to spare her the pain of seeing Lily die and for that she was also grateful. She had not been to see Lily since the day her mama had died, and had neither seen nor spoken to Joseph. Her father had visited Lily's family and they had told him of her worsening condition.

It was time to go. They had packed what little items of clothing they had purchased over the past weeks and some provisions for the long journey ahead. As they were leaving for the port, their goodbyes to Mr Darwin were strained. He gave Harriet a small book which she took without speaking, although she knew he would not be offended. Miss Wedgewood came to see them off and she hugged Harriet and wished her luck.

They had to make a change to their route.

Papa said that a last minute problem had arisen. Although he had taken care of all the details regarding March Lane, there was somebody he needed to meet with briefly and though she was alarmed at the thought of seeing her home again, she said it would be alright because she wanted to appear brave and grown up for him.

And so she was sat in the carriage in the lane, waiting for her papa. She could not look in the direction of the house at first but when she glanced at it only fleetingly it suddenly felt like something inside her had collapsed. Like an elastic pulled too tightly that suddenly snaps – she finally began to cry. Her tears began slowly but then she had to bite her handkerchief to prevent the driver from hearing her sobs.

After a very long time she could cry no more. She slumped against the carriage seat wishing that her papa would hurry. When she saw him coming back from the house he was talking in a hushed voice to a policeman. He was a tall, slim man with a hat that made him appear even taller. The carriage door was not quite closed and they were unaware that their conversation carried to her.

'You do understand now, sir, why we think what we do?'

'Yes constable. This makes the situation even more distressing and convinces me that I am doing the right thing by leaving.'

'You may be right. Word is that they got in through the kitchen door. We have managed to apprehend one of the men and he gave us some information. He says the door was open.'

Harriet gasped.

'Says they were paid to go and start the fire in the study. He also says it was because of some papers, they weren't told what they were, that they were just doing someone else's dirty work. Then they hoofed it out of there once the fire was set.'

'When we first spoke I told you that's what I believed the fire to be about: those papers were important, to do with my work...' Her papa's voice was strained. 'My wife, she wouldn't be dead if it were not for...'

The policeman interrupted him gently, 'We will find who did this. We aren't far off getting them. Whether they were important papers or not is of no matter to the police.

It's the crimes of breaking and entering, arson and your wife's murder.'

Harriet heard her father make a small choking sound, as though trying to contain his emotions.

After a long pause he said, 'What I still can't understand is how the kitchen door could have been open. Wickes was meticulous in ensuring everything was locked up at night.'

'We spoke to him and he says he locked the door and put the key in its usual place on the shelf. It's a bit of a mystery.'

Harriet felt sick. It was her fault! She had left the kitchen door unlocked when she went in search of the journals and when she had come back to the house somebody had been inside.

She had been responsible.

She had killed Mama!

CHAPTER TWENTY-NINE

Flora felt so guilty at the thought of lying to her dad again that she finally told him where she was going, although she did bend the truth a little.

'Would it be alright for me to go to the yard in a bit, Dad?' she'd asked as they ate their tea at the kitchen table.

Her dad stopped eating, 'Why's that?'

'I want to check on Colin. He didn't seem like himself today and I've been worried about him.'

'Really? He was fine when I left him, eating his dinner as quickly as Usain Bolt runs the hundred metres.'

'I know, but I just want to make sure.'

Her dad ate a mouthful of food, then said, 'If it's bothering you I'll drive you round later.'

'No, you don't have to. You look really tired. Archie will come with me. We'll only pop round to see him, then we'll come straight home.'

'It'll be dark, Flora. You know I wouldn't let you do that.'

'Dad, come on, it's just around the corner and I have my phone. I know it's dark but it's early evening, if it was summer if would still be light. I won't be long. Plus you've still got those accounts to do. I'll be safe with Archie,' Flora thought she sounded a bit too desperate, and she was sure her dad would suspect something.

'You're a daft one for that dog, Flora but as long as you phone me when you get there and when you're leaving… you can go. I do have to get those invoices sorted – and I suppose I've got to let you do some things on your own,' he said sadly.

Flora felt guilty. She reached for his hand. 'I know Dad, I'll be there and back before you realise that I'm gone.' She stood up to take her plate to the dishwasher and kissed his head as she passed him. She was glad he was her dad.

Mable was waiting for them outside the yard when they arrived. She got out of her little blue car and came over to them, a weak smile on her face. She seemed like a different person, small and frail, her face drawn. Flora wondered again if they were doing the right thing.

'Hello. How are you, Mable?' asked Flora tentatively.

'I'm alright. I'm sorry if this seems strange to you both, but I've been doing some soul searching this past week and if it's alright with you, I would like to see the room where you found the tile floor.'

Flora nodded, 'I thought that's what you wanted to see, but why are you being so secretive?'

'I will tell you, if I'm right. I promise.' Her gaze was so direct that Flora believed her.

'I just have to call my dad before we go in,' said Flora taking her phone from her pocket. The last thing she wanted was her dad hurrying around to the warehouse because she hadn't phoned. Once she had reassured him she was safe and wouldn't be long she hung up, unlocked the gate and turned to Mable.

'The yard belongs to Colin at night. He might be a bit wary of you. He'll probably growl but he'll listen to me when I tell him, so don't be frightened.'

As Flora had said, they heard Colin's low growl before they saw him.

Flora called out, 'It's me boy. Come here.'

Colin bounded out of the darkness towards Flora. His tail was whipping furiously back and forth but when he saw Mable he stopped so suddenly that he skidded.

Flora was astonished.

Cowering as close to the floor as he could with his ears flat against his head, Colin made his way to Mable until he was at her feet, then he rolled over in complete submission. Mable bent down and smoothed Colin gently on the stomach, speaking so quietly to him that Flora couldn't hear what she was saying. Colin whimpered as he sat up then gently wagged his tail.

Archie couldn't believe it. He'd known Colin since he'd been a small fluffy pup but he was still very aware that he was a guard dog of the most ferocious breed. He raised his eyebrows and Flora lifted her shoulders in reply; she'd never seen anything like it.

Mable smiled at them both. 'You best lead the way, Flora. You stay here, Colin. Good boy,' Mable said softly and Colin obediently lay down.

Flora was still shocked but turned and went to open the warehouse doors. As they passed through them she glanced behind her briefly and saw Colin with his head resting on his paws.

They climbed the stairs to the third floor. Archie had brought his torch and the light pierced the darkness. The warehouse felt uneasy to Flora, as though it was holding its breath, waiting for something. Every noise they made as they ascended the old staircase echoed in the big space and it made Flora feel nervous.

When they reached the tile room Flora pulled on the light switch. The bulb cast a dull light on the centre of the room but the corners remained in shadow.

'Do you want to see the floor, Mable?' Archie asked, not really sure what they could show her. The last they'd seen of the tiles they were smashed into tiny pieces and he had no idea where they were now.

'No thank you Archie, but I wouldn't mind a chair if you could get me one.'

'Okay.' Archie quickly headed to the room he knew to be full of old furniture. He didn't want to be alone any longer than he needed to. He grabbed a dusty antique chair, the closest to him, and hurried back.

Mable sat down, looking around the room as she did.

'I suppose we should wait now,' Mable sighed.

Flora suddenly realised what Mable wanted to do. 'I'm not sure it works like that. If you're waiting for the ghost to appear, it won't. It just left the clues. We felt it's presence but it didn't show itself to us. Even when it spoke to Archie...'

'…we didn't actually see it,' said Archie interrupting her. Mable was trying to do the very thing that he and Flora had decided against.

'I don't think this is a good idea. It could be dangerous. I think we should leave.' Archie glared at Flora desperately.

'It's me!' Mable suddenly said very loudly but not to Flora and Archie who were both suddenly glued to the floor.

'I'm here!' Mable called again.

'Stop! Please!' Archie begged Mable.

'Oh please don't worry, Archie. No one will hurt you. If it is who I think it is you will be quite safe,' she said gently.

'I'm leaving,' said Archie moving quickly towards the door, he grabbed Flora's hand as he passed her but as he did so the bulb flickered above them. He stopped and looked at Flora, horrified. Flora didn't want to be alone in the corridor and, although she felt threatened now, she knew that there was safety in numbers. She pulled Archie with her until their backs were against the wall. They watched as the bulb stuttered again.

'Is that you?' Mable called. 'I know it is… It must be you.'

The exposed bulb began to move, swinging backwards and forwards then around and around in a fast circular motion. All that Flora and Archie could do was watch, terrified.

'Please. I must see you. I must know that it *is* you!' Mable called out again.

Then the light went out.

Flora's chest was thumping and she could feel Archie's

hand squeezing hers so tightly she thought he might break every bone. She heard his laboured breathing which she now understood was a symptom of his fear. In the darkness there was a shuffling and Flora was so frightened that she thought she was going to faint. Then the light came back on again and Flora sucked in a sharp breath as Archie gasped.

Standing in front of Mable was a girl.

CHAPTER THIRTY

If Flora had not already known it, if she had walked into the room unexpectedly, she would have believed that the girl facing Mable was real. She wasn't transparent as she'd imagined ghosts to look; in fact she appeared to be as alive as both her and Archie, apart from two things. Her lack of colour and a delicate, wispy halo of light that glowed around her silhouette. The girl's clothing was black and white and her face, hands and hair, varying shades of grey. She was dressed in a white pinafore over an ankle length dress and wore dark buttoned boots on her feet. She looked as though she had stepped from the pages of a Charles Dickens novel or an old black and white photograph.

Flora and Archie were stood side on to the girl and Mable. Flora could feel Archie shaking and her stomach was flip-flopping over and over. They were watching this strange tableau, when the girl turned to them. Flora felt Archie stiffen next to her. The girl observed them curiously for a moment and then she smiled.

'Hello, Archie. I'm sorry if I frightened you when I spoke to you,' she said with such sweet sadness that Flora felt it pull inside her chest. The girl's voice was not inside the room, but echoed in Flora's head. Flora glanced at Archie and Mable and knew that they had heard the girl in their heads too, it was such a strange sensation that Flora shivered.

'Um... hello,' Archie said. He sounded too loud.

The girl turned back to Mable.

'Is it really you? You look so... old,' she said and though the girl's lips moved, again her voice was inside their heads.

'That's because I *am* old,' Mable stated and began to cry.

The girl took a step forward then knelt in front of Mable.

'Oh! It *is* you! Your voice sounds different but your eyes – they are exactly the same! Please don't cry. My friend...' And then Flora and Archie both caught their breath again as the girl reached out and took Mable's hand.

They watched and listened in stunned silence.

'It's been so very long, Harriet!' Mable said through her tears.

'It has and I have missed you Lily but you must stop crying now. I have much to tell you and so little time.'

Archie looked at Flora – L stood for Lily! But why was the ghost-girl calling Mable – Lily?

Mable pulled a handkerchief from her sleeve and wiped her eyes. The girl was still kneeling and once Mable's face was dry she took her hand again.

'I have dreamed about this, about meeting you again but didn't ever believe it could happen. If it had not been for these wonderful children coming to the house about the tile floor...' Mable's voice trailed off as she glanced from Flora to Archie and then back to the girl.

'It was the only way that I could lead you to me. I cannot leave. I was never able to come to you, so I had to think of a way to bring you to me.' The girl then spoke to Flora and Archie, 'Thank you both, and you really are a great detective Flora – but there is one more thing that you will need to do before this mystery is complete,' she said.

Flora nodded and blushed, unable to speak.

'Now I shall begin – at the end – and perhaps your questions will finally be answered my dear Lily.'

'When we left for New Zealand, I was devastated. I had overheard Papa being told by the police constable that the unlocked kitchen door had allowed the arsonists to get into our home. Your mother had told Papa that you were close to death and would live only a few more days. It was my fault that Mama was dead and I blamed myself for yours too.

'You see, I had gone into the garden that night to retrieve the journal. I had found them in a sack in the glass house during the day but had only managed to briefly read three of them when Papa almost caught me. I planned to collect the last one that night, take it to my room to read, then return it before Papa took them. It was me that left the kitchen door open. I gave entrance to those awful men who set fire to our home!'

Harriet stopped, her voice was small and so very sad. She breathed in deeply, 'When we boarded the ship I was in such a terrible state of mind. The guilt was overwhelming me and I could not even share it with Papa.

'After several weeks at sea I caught a fever. Just knowing that I was responsible for everything that had happened, to Mama, to you, made me very ill. My health deteriorated and I died on the ship. After my death, my father disembarked with my body at the next port.

'It was a small island in the South Seas with just one village. The kind people saw Papa's distress and offered him a place to stay. I was buried there and he stayed and became a recluse. He asked the ship's captain to keep his whereabouts secret until he came to terms with his grief, and promised to join the next ship that sailed to the island.

'But dear Papa did not live long after me. I think losing Mama and then me in such a short space of time was too much for him to bare, and in less than a year his heart gave up, just as poor Mama's did, and he died.'

Both Harriet and Mable were very distressed.

'That was why there was no news. No one could understand it. For months we tried to find out what had happened to you, if you had made it to New Zealand safely but despite the letters that were sent even your father's solicitors could not find a trace.'

'Papa settled all his affairs before we left for our new life; his solicitors knew nothing of my death and had no knowledge that he had left the ship before we reached New Zealand. And when he died the secret remained. The captain of our ship was an honourable man and obviously kept to his word. And there was, after all, no family left alive to pursue anything with regards to his estate.'

'Oh, Harriet. I am so very sorry.' Mable said sadly.

'It is a tragic tale. But now thanks to Flora and Archie we are reunited. You are still alive after all this time and here we are two friends together at last,' said Harriet.

Mable agreed, 'That's true, although living for such a long time has not been easy.' She paused, 'But how do you know about those things? The things that happened *after* your death? And how did you come to be here?'

'I really don't know. The occurrences after my death are like a distant dream. I can't explain it. I just know that that is what happened to my dear Papa... and to me. It is a strange, unnerving thing. It's like having a memory of an event that I was never involved in. The question as to why I am here I finally have the answer to, because *you* are sitting in front of me!

'This building is a home to many, we are drawn to it. It may be because we have a purpose that we did not conclude when we were living, so we stay and wait with an item that once belonged to us and links us to our past life. That is the reason I am here, so perhaps that is the case for the others.'

The whole building was crowded with ghosts? Flora could hardly believe it!

'Now you know my story you must tell me yours,' Harriet said quietly.

Mable cleared her throat then began.

'As you can see, I did recover. It took almost three months in hospital, by which time you and your papa had gone. When the doctors finally removed the bandages the burns and the scars had disappeared. Not a mark remained on my skin and my hair had grown back. I was a miracle patient! No one could believe it or understand it, no one except Joseph. He was at my bedside almost every day and when I was finally well enough to leave the hospital he visited me at home. He told me what had happened in the garden after your papa had rescued me. He said that you gave me something – but he had no idea what it was.

'Whilst I was in the hospital he too believed that I was going to die, so he went back to March Lane for the sack. He knew that there were several books inside it and was hoping to find the answer to what you had given me but when he got there it was gone. That area of garden nearest to the house had caught alight and the place where you had hidden the sack was burned to dust. The sack and the answers were destroyed by the fire too.

'The doctors were asking questions about my miraculous healing, they wanted to use me as a specimen, and soon some newspaper men heard my story. It was all too much! Joe asked me if I would go to Canada with him. He had heard that land was being given away in the French colonies for people who wanted to work it. It was an opportunity to begin a new life. So I stayed in hiding with my sister, Gwener and as soon as I was old enough Joe and I were married and we left for Canada.'

'You married Joe?!' Harriet squealed 'That's so... so romantic. I think I was a little bit in love with him myself!'

Mable smiled, 'Well that doesn't surprise me. He was everything that was good and kind.' Then she frowned, 'I miss him even now.'

'What happened in Canada?'

'We lived in the Northern Territories. It was a beautiful place, although when winter came it was unlike any winter we had ever experienced at home. But we had never seen so much open space and such an expanse of sky. It was beautiful. We built a cabin and bought some cattle with money that Joe had saved and we grew vegetables and corn. It wasn't easy, it was a harsh existence at times but we were happy and content to be living it together.'

Mable stopped for a moment as if she was remembering something painful. 'It was Joe's thirty-fifth birthday and I was tidying my hair in a looking-glass and it suddenly dawned on me that my appearance was no different from the day I had married him almost sixteen years earlier. Joe put it down to the fresh air and healthy life, but it soon became clear to me that I simply wasn't aging. Sometime later, an Irish family passed through and we offered them a place on our land for the night. When Joe introduced me they thought I was his daughter. We explained that I was only two years younger than him but they didn't believe us. It was a horrible experience.

'We were lucky though, we had very few visitors and our nearest neighbours were too far from us to know, but if ever we were in company... we took to pretending to be father and daughter. Those were the saddest times for me.

'Joe didn't know what you had given me. He said it had been too dark and all he saw was you tipping something into my mouth and then of course, neither of us spoke to you ever again. We guessed it had something to do with Mr

Darwin, but that remains a mystery even now. I remember that I didn't speak to you at all that day before the fire. Joe said he'd found the sack of journals in the garden shed, and then in the glass house a few days before the fire but he didn't read them. There were many times over the years when he'd wished he had. He knew you must have read them.' Mable stopped, 'Joe passed away in his sixtieth year.'

'Oh, Lily! I am so, so sorry. Poor Joe, poor you!'

Mable's voice was strained as she continued, 'With Joe gone I stayed on the land and I realised that I *was* beginning to age but in a different, much slower way. Five years was like a single year to me. Eventually I had to leave our cabin and our land. The countryside was becoming more populated and developed into towns that were growing into cities. It was dangerous and difficult for a girl alone, so I decided it would be safer if I left but it broke my heart.

'I began to move around Canada. I lived in places only long enough that people wouldn't realise that I wasn't getting older. I went west to Vancouver, then east to Kitchener. Always moving. When I reached what might have been my late-twenties it was easier, the world had changed and women alone were accepted much more. Joe and I had saved some money and I got a large settlement from the sale of our land, so I enrolled at a Canadian university part-time and studied for a degree. I became a history teacher. That was the easy part. I had lived the history that I was teaching and no matter how old you are children will always see you as just another grown up. I travelled and I taught, but it was a lonely life never staying in one place for too long, not making friends for fear that they would discover my secret. Then a few years ago I had finally had enough, I was weary from the strain of living such a solitary life, so I decided to come home.'

Archie couldn't believe what he was hearing. Mable who was apparently Lily was telling a ghost called Harriet that she was almost two hundred years old! He wondered if he was going mad.

'So all this time you had no idea how you were healed, or why you didn't age as other people did?' Harriet asked.

'Joe and I assumed I was cured because of what you gave to me, but only because you said it would make me better. I knew a little about Mr Darwin's findings because of the conversation I'd overheard in the study, but nothing more than that.

'Much later, we wrote to Mr Darwin when we realised what was happening to me, not explaining the exact reasons we were writing in case anyone read the letter, but we didn't receive a reply. I learned everything I could about Charles Darwin later in my life but I found nothing that ever mentioned the mysterious research and diaries from that time. His journals from his travels are still held in the Natural History Museum in London, so the notes that you found were something altogether different.'

'Then that is the reason we are here; why I am here! It's why I left the clues for Flora and Archie,' Harriet said cheerfully.

'What do you mean?' Mable asked frowning.

'I gave you some seeds!'

'Seeds?' Mable said puzzled.

'Mr Darwin left some seeds in a glass pot. When I read his journals in the glass house, Mr Darwin had written that he'd collected the seeds on his travels, but from exactly where he didn't say, or perhaps I skipped that part because his writing was so difficult to read. He travelled the world, so they could have come from anywhere. He said that the seeds had healed some mice he had been testing but I didn't read further because Papa came along and interrupted me. That was why I went to the garden that night, to retrieve the last journal, only I didn't get the chance to read it. In the chaos of the fire and when I saw how badly hurt you were, I gave the seeds to you in desperation.'

Mable's face had grown pale.

'And I know where Mr Darwin's final journal is, the journal that explains everything; the one that I took from the sack in the garden,' said Harriet.

'What do you mean? The journals were all burned, lost in the fire when it spread to the garden,' Mable stated.

'The journals that were in the sack are gone – but not the last one! It's my destiny! I am in this warehouse to conclude the final piece of *your* mystery!' Harriet's excited voice was loud inside their heads. 'I took the journal from the sack in the garden back to the house but I was too tired to read it so I put it inside the secret drawer in my wardrobe. I thought it was destroyed in the fire... but it wasn't. It was only when I became aware of being here that I knew. I am linked to the wardrobe as well as to the tile floor; I am connected to Mr Darwin's journal and my own

169

diary – as they both still remain inside the wardrobe!'

Mable's eyes were wide, 'The wardrobe? It's here? I thought everything had burned...' and then she stopped. 'Of course, the ground floor was all but gone, but some of the upstairs rooms remained.' Her voice was suddenly high with anticipation. 'Quickly, Harriet, where is it? Take me to it.'

'It was here until three days ago. The wardrobe has gone and I am fearful that I will find myself in the place that it now resides and you will never know anything further unless we hurry,' said Harriet quietly.

CHAPTER THIRTY-ONE

Harriet turned to Flora and Archie who had stood against the wall and listened to the entire account. If they hadn't been talking to a ghost, Mable's story about living for almost two hundred years would have seemed too far-fetched to ever consider, but now the girl came silently towards them.

Archie's hand in Flora's was still shaking.

'I'm sorry, I have not introduced myself,' said the ghost girl. 'I am Harriet Mathias. It is nice to meet you both at last.' Harriet's gaze held theirs and Flora felt like she was being pulled into a long bright tunnel. The girl from the drawing looked at her, her eyes wide.

'I am going to need your help urgently,' she said.

Flora stuttered, 'Anything. What... do... you... want... us... to... do?'

Harriet smiled gently, 'There is nothing to be afraid of, Flora. If it wasn't for you I would never have seen my friend Lily again. But I will tell you quickly. I fear time is getting away from us.' She sounded both very young and very old at the same time.

Flora nodded, worried that if she spoke again her squeaky voice would give her away.

'A man came three days ago, a man who resembled a

ferret. He was highly unpleasant. He came with your father and bought some furniture from him. He saw my wardrobe and I knew that he realised its worth as an antique. Although your father knew it too, he sold it to the man because your father is a good soul. The man has taken the wardrobe but I do not know where. You have to find it and open the secret drawer. I left the key for the lock on your last visit. The wardrobe has been here a very long time. I did not think that it would ever be sold.'

Archie spoke this time, surprising Flora, 'Of course we'll help. It's Mr Wessel that bought the wardrobe.' His voice was shaking too as he turned to Flora. 'Your dad said he was going to give him a ring about selling some furniture. He's probably taken it back to his shop, but I'm not sure how we can get to the drawer without him realising what we are doing.'

Flora thought for a moment. 'We have to get into his shop.' Flora felt determined to help, even more so as Harriet had been so kind about her dad.

Mable stood up, 'Perhaps that's where I can help. I can go to the shop and buy the wardrobe back from this Mr Wessel.'

Archie nodded, 'We could come with you to show you where the shop is.'

'I'm sure I could find it, but if you come I would certainly be grateful for the company. You'd have to stay out of sight though. We don't want him to become suspicious.'

'We could go in the morning,' Archie said. 'We'd have

to have an excuse not to be at school 'til later. That's easy for me. What about you Flora?'

'I'll think of something to tell my dad,' Flora said.

'That's settled then. We'll go to the shop in the morning. I'll buy the wardrobe and arrange for it to be delivered to March Lane. If I get a chance I could always try and see if I can open the drawer,' Mable said.

'You'd need a lot of time. He's always in the shop alone and rarely lets any customer's out of his sight. It's probably best not to risk it,' said Flora, her courage growing.

Harriet went to Mable and hugged her – a real hug that made the tears come back to Mable's eyes.

Flora couldn't believe it. How could a ghost touch anything? But then how could they even be talking to a ghost? She had a hundred questions.

'I will see you soon, Lily. Come back to see me when it is done. We will talk again...' then Harriet began to fade and with a cold draught that swirled around them, she was gone.

'Can you believe what just happened?' Archie asked Flora. Both of them were still in shock.

They were back at Flora's house sitting with their backs against the warm radiator in her bedroom. Thankfully Flora's dad hadn't noticed how long they'd been gone, he was still busy sorting out his paperwork downstairs in their small study, although she had done as he'd asked and phoned him twice.

'Not really. It all seems a bit too far-fetched. I mean if I hadn't been there...' replied Flora.

'And the fact that a ghost actually appeared,' Archie was still wobbly about what they had just experienced.

'And spoke to us!' interrupted Flora.

'What about Mable being a hundred and ninety-two! What did you make of that?' asked Archie.

'It's too weird! When she explained about being a housemaid and that she'd been responsible for cleaning the tile floor twice a day I could hardly believe it! When we turned up out of the blue asking about the floor she obviously knew that something strange was going on,' said Flora.

'She was a pretty good actress though.'

'It sounds like she's had to be. Living that long without anyone finding out, you'd have to be a good "teller of tall tales", as my dad says.'

'And then that stuff about the drawing. That was too spooky!' said Archie.

Mable had told them that the drawing that had fallen out of the album was hers.

Just before she'd left for Canada with Joseph she had gone back to March Lane. She'd found the drawing in the downstairs ruins of the house and had kept it safe through all the years. It was always in a locked jewellery box in her bedroom. When Flora discovered it, Mable had to try very hard to hold herself together. She had no explanation as to how it got inside the album.

'I'm finding it *all* difficult to believe. Those things they said about Charles Darwin, they actually knew him. It's strangely exciting, don't you think?' The more Flora thought about it the more exhilarated she felt.

'Yeah I suppose it is – in a completely freaked out sort of way. Mable must have seen an awful lot if she is that old. I wish we'd had a chance to speak to her properly instead of hurrying back here,' Archie sighed.

'Me too, but I didn't want my dad coming round to the warehouse. Anyway, we'll have a chance to ask her tomorrow and at least we've solved some of the clues we had. The letter L is for Lily, the tile floor *was* from March Lane – it obviously didn't come to us from the builder but I expect if we went through the very early ledgers we would find an entry for it; it was probably in the warehouse before dad was even born. And the little brass key opens a hidden drawer in Harriet's wardrobe!' Flora smiled.

'I was wondering: if she has kept her secret for so long, how come she didn't mind *us* knowing it?' asked Archie.

'I suppose she really didn't have a choice. Once we told her about the haunting she made the connection and there were really too many messages for her to ignore.'

'Do you think she trusts us not to tell anyone?'

'Who would believe us if we did tell?' Flora laughed.

'Yeah, you're right! The answer to that would be no one,' said Archie with a grin.

CHAPTER THIRTY-TWO

'Dad, would it be alright if I go into school a bit late today?' Flora walked into the kitchen dressed in her school uniform.

'Why's that?' her dad looked up from his paper and cup of tea.

'I just want to go to the library and pick up a few books.' Flora felt that she'd been telling so many lies to her dad that at any moment her nose would begin to grow.

'Can't you do that after school?'

'I could for some of the books but I need one for a lesson this afternoon and I just wanted to prove to Mrs Stone that I'd got it.'

'This afternoon! You're cutting it a bit fine, aren't you? You're always lecturing me on how disorganised I am with my book work, perhaps you should listen to your own advice.'

'Is that a yes then?' Flora smiled her most persuasive smile.

'Well just this once. I'll ring the school and tell them, but next time remember – fail to prepare, prepare to fail!' He shook his head as he went back to reading his paper.

Flora laughed as she grabbed her coat and school bag from the banister, and then raced out of the house. When this adventure was over she promised herself that she would sit down with her dad and tell him everything.

Mable collected Flora and Archie from outside Archie's house. Flora knew his mum wouldn't be in and it made no difference if he was late for school. They climbed into the back of Mable's car and made their way towards town.

Flora was itching to ask Mable a million questions but Archie jumped in first.

'So Mable are you really two hundred years old?'

'Get to the point, why don't you?' said Flora, giving Archie a nudge.

'Well not quite, Archie. I'm a hundred and ninety-two to be precise.'

There was a moment of silence. Even though they had already discussed it, Flora and Archie still couldn't believe what they were hearing.

'I was born on the 30th of April, 1823 and it seems such a very long time ago,' said Mable with a sigh.

'Should we call you Mable or Lily?' asked Archie.

'Lily was the name I was given when I was born, Lily Martin. Evans is my married surname. I took my mother's name, Mable, when I moved away to Canada. There were too many people asking questions about my recovery and we didn't want anyone following us to our new life. Joe always called me Lily but I was Mable to everyone else from then on, so I think you should continue to call me Mable.'

'Did your mother know about your long life?' Flora

didn't know what else to call it.

'No. We kept in touch by letter but they were few and far between. The post wasn't like it is now and the world was different then, once we'd left our home behind we never saw our families again.'

'And it was the seeds that Harriet gave you that have made you live so long?' said Flora.

'And stopped you from growing old normally?' said Archie.

'Yes – it seems as though it was.'

'Where did the seeds come from?' asked Flora.

'That is what I'm hoping to find out. I overheard a conversation between Mr Darwin and the master, Mr Mathias. They were discussing a discovery, something that was so wonderful but that the world wasn't ready for. Mr Darwin believed it was terribly dangerous, and that society, at that time, would not readily accept such a discovery, that was why Mr Mathias took the journals for safekeeping.

'You have probably heard about Charles Darwin's book, *On the Origin of Species*, and his theories about evolution. The other journals were obviously something altogether different from that.

'I've read all that I could since that time and the Internet is a marvellous way to find things out. I wanted some clues as to why I have lived so long, but all I found was that Mr Darwin travelled the world and brought back many specimens of plants, birds and animals. He published books on his *Beagle Journeys* but in all of my searching I haven't discovered anything about this other research.

'I had a think about it last night, and went through my old notes now that I know what Harriet gave to me but I still found nothing. I have no idea where those particular seeds came from, or which plant, or even if there is a cure. I am hoping that the journal hidden in the wardrobe will shed some light on that,' said Mable sounding very sad.

Flora had never thought of living so long as an illness that could be cured. The possibility of immortality always seemed so exciting, but now she could see how lonely Mable must be.

As if reading her thoughts Archie said, 'It must have been difficult for you being alone all that time; not to have anyone to talk to or share your secret with.'

'Very hard indeed, Archie, but I have a feeling you know something of that.' She looked at him in the rear view mirror and he smiled sadly at her.

'What's it like living so long?' he asked.

'It has its bad points, but some good things have happened to me along the way too. It's not all doom, gloom and misery you know.'

'If you could find a cure, would you really take it?' asked Flora seriously.

'Now that's a question I have asked myself since my beloved Joe died and I'm still not sure I have the answer.' Mable sighed again.

The sat nav interrupted them to announce that they had reached their destination. Flora pointed out Mr Wessel's shop as they drove past looking for a parking space along the high street. Once they had stopped a safe distance away

Mable turned to Flora and Archie in the back of the car. 'So what can you tell me that might be useful?' she asked.

'The shop is on two floors. Upstairs he keeps all the furniture that is small and easier to move, tables, chairs, old chests, things like that. The big stuff is downstairs, that's where the wardrobe will be,' Flora said.

'Right then. You two stay here and I'll see what I can do,' she smiled at them as she got out of the car.

Mable was surprised to see a neat shop front. The bricks had been painted white and the woodwork and windows were washed clean. It wasn't to her taste but it gave the impression of someone that was proud of his place of work. The dark green front door was to the right of a large window that reached the pavement. Displayed on a small platform in the window were two leather winged chairs and a mahogany side table. An old, leather-bound book lay open on one of the chairs as if its reader had just popped away for a moment. Very tasteful, Mable thought, and perhaps not such an easy man to fool.

A brass plaque on the wall read *Wessel's Antiques and Curiosities est. 1900,* that too was shining as if it had just been polished. She wasn't sure if her hand shook with excitement or trepidation as she went inside.

Mr Wessel was in front of her before she had even closed the door; in fact, as she turned to close it he shut it for her.

'Good morning, madam. How may I help you?'

Mable now understood exactly what Harriet had been

talking about when she'd described him.

Mr Wessel was a tall man with greasy hair swept back from his receding hairline. He was bone thin to the point of being skeletal and his eyes were so close together that they made him look just like a weasel, although, she thought, that was being quite unkind to weasels. He reminded Mable of the money lenders that she had sometimes seen in the city when she was a child. There was something sly about him, but also an air of intelligence. She would have to put on her best performance if she was to convince this man that she was a genuine customer.

'Good morning,' said Mable, holding out her hand, despite the feeling that she wanted to be as far away from his clammy handshake. She boldly continued with her charade. 'I wish to purchase an item of furniture. A wardrobe, a large one to be exact.'

'Of course, madam. You have come to the right place. Let me show you what I currently have in stock.' His voice was as greasy as his hair.

For the first time Mable inspected the room. It was bigger than it had seemed from outside, more than double the size and over-crowded with antiques: beds, chest of drawers, sofas and decrepit pianos that seemed too old for anyone to play again.

'This way please,' Mr Wessel said as he weaved his way through the numerous antiques towards several wardrobes that were all together under the stairs.

Mable immediately recognised the wardrobe, *Harriet's wardrobe* and she had to hide her shock.

'This one is particularly large,' he said walking past the wardrobe to a huge ebony monstrosity.

'Mmm, I'm not sure. The wood is too dark. I do however like this one,' Mable said pointing to the one she was really interested in.

'I'm sorry, madam but that has just been sold,' Mr Wessel said with a sly grin.

Mable's heart raced. 'Oh really? What a shame. That would sit so well in my bedroom. May I ask how much you've sold it for?'

'Madam, I can't possibly divulge such a thing…'

'Only… well, never mind. I'm afraid there really is nothing of any interest beside this one,' Mable pretended disinterest and began to walk towards the door.

'It is very expensive,' Mr Wessel said loudly across the room. Mable stopped and turned around.

'I'm sure it is,' Mable said, 'but perhaps I can match what you've sold it for with perhaps… an extra ten percent?'

Mable watched as Mr Wessel appeared to be wrestling with his conscience. 'I'm not sure, the buyers will be so disappointed, but perhaps twenty-five percent. That would make it one thousand nine hundred pounds.'

He stared at Mable, and she had the strangest feeling that he knew why she was so desperate to buy it. Should she carry on the charade? She certainly couldn't walk away. She was in a dilemma.

She called his bluff.

'One thousand seven hundred and pounds,' she said boldly.

'One thousand eight hundred,' and he held out his hand to shake on the price.

Mable hesitated for a moment then reluctantly took it. 'I would like delivery included,' she demanded and Mr Wessel grimaced before nodding his consent.

CHAPTER THIRTY-THREE

Flora and Archie couldn't stay in the car, they were far too fidgety. Instead they loitered across the road from the shop trying to keep out of sight. The large front window allowed them to see inside and they watched as Mable had a brief conversation with Mr Wessel before moving towards the back.

They didn't have to wait long before Mable came out of the shop and hurried along the pavement where they caught up with her.

She unlocked the car and the three of them got in.

'I did it. It was so peculiar seeing that old wardrobe again,' she sighed heavily, 'Anyway, I bargained with him but it wasn't easy. He was very unpleasant and I had a strange feeling that he knew why I wanted it.'

'I told you he wasn't nice. But there's no way he could know anything,' said Flora.

'Yes you're right, and he *was* horrible; a greedy little man who reminded me of a certain Mr Scrooge. And there was something menacing about him. How your father could do business with someone like that I don't know.' Mable looked at her watch. 'We'd better get moving. I'll drop you off at school on my way home.'

'Will it be delivered?' Archie asked.

'Yes, on Saturday. He said that he would send a van at midday.'

'Can we come to your house then?' Flora asked.

'Of course! I couldn't have done this without you both. You need to know the end of this story as much I do. After all, if it wasn't for you and Archie, well... you know. I can come and collect you around ten on Saturday.'

Flora could see how emotional Mable was; it showed on her face.

'It's a bit of a journey to come and get us then bring us back. Are you sure it's alright?' Flora said though only half-heartedly, she was desperate to know if the journal was still inside the wardrobe.

'It's fine. It's been so nice to have my days filled up like this for a change and to have some people in my life who actually know the truth,' then she said in an almost child-like way, 'You won't tell anyone about me will you?'

Archie and Flora both laughed. 'We've already had that discussion and we decided that no one would ever believe us!' said Archie.

Mable laughed too, 'I suppose you're right, it's quite a story isn't it?'

She started the car and they pulled away from the high street. Flora gave her directions to their school. When they reached the gates they gathered their school bags, got out and said goodbye.

'I'll see you on Saturday morning. Bye.' And with that she drove away.

Flora and Archie watched the car disappear.

'It's so exciting,' Flora grinned, 'I can hardly think. I'm dying to know if the journal is there and what it actually says. I'm not sure I can make it through until Saturday!'

'You'll make it,' he said rolling his eyes. 'Come on, we'd better move before we get detention!'

Solomon Wessel looked out of his shop window at the woman who had just bought the wardrobe from him. He watched as she scurried along the pavement and then disappeared out of sight.

Something wasn't right. He'd had a feeling from the minute she'd walked through the door that she wasn't what she appeared to be. He was good at seeing through people, it was how he'd stayed in business for so long. He also knew how to get things from them. Most people were naturally stupid.

Take the wardrobe – he'd known its value and had seen it at Horace Theodore's place months ago. He'd had his eye on it and foolish Theodore hadn't even realised its worth and let it go for a song. He'd paid sixty pounds for it. He'd made an extremely good profit today. But he was sure the woman knew it wasn't worth what she paid for it, so why had she parted with almost two thousand pounds? At most it was worth five hundred.

And of course there was no other buyer; the "interested party" was always a good ruse to make people pay over the odds. Wessel's clever mind for business was the reason for the ever-growing piles of cash hidden under his mattress.

He went to the door, bolted it and turned the 'Open'

sign to 'Closed.' He never usually shut the shop during the day, everyone who walked through the door was a potential way to make even more money, but today he made an exception.

He walked to the back and stood in front of the wardrobe that he'd just sold for almost four times its worth. Was it just luck or was there really something about this piece of furniture that he'd missed? That woman had wanted it badly, despite her pretence that she wasn't really bothered.

Why?

He stood and pondered, rubbing his chin.

He opened the doors. The space was large but a sickly, spicy smell wafted towards him. He screwed up his nose with distaste. He cast his eyes around the inside, not really sure what he was expecting to see. It appeared to be just an empty cupboard. He quickly closed the doors, glad to be rid of the smell that was now leaving a rancid taste in his mouth. He paced around inspecting the outside of the wardrobe, tapping his knuckles along the wood as he went. Nothing. No secret opening.

He returned once more to the doors. He wasn't going to open them again, the pungent smell inside was already making him feel nauseous.

Perhaps for the first time he'd been wrong, there was no ulterior motive, just a stupid woman with no idea how she was spending her money.

He smiled; it was his lucky day after all.

CHAPTER THIRTY-FOUR

High up in the farthest corner of the darkest room in the warehouse, Harriet waited. She could hear the comings and goings of people and everyday life three floors below: Flora's father conducting his business, customers arriving and asking for help. She yearned for the company of real people – people who lived and breathed.

She shifted slightly and then she was in the tile room, the place where her idea had begun. She sighed as she floated like a leaf on the wind around the room. It would soon be over and perhaps she would be able to leave at last, she could hardly wait – but a part of her was still fearful of what was to come. Would Mama be waiting for her? Would she blame her for the terrible fire? Would Papa be there too, holding out his arms to draw the three of them together as he had done when he had stepped from the train at the station?

She liked the warehouse; it had been her home for many years and she was never completely alone, but she longed to be with her family.

She closed her eyes and in a blink she appeared in another dusty room. The room held many items of antique furniture. When she finally settled – it was not sitting or standing, as she could do neither, she just simply *was* – she closed her eyes and wished for Lily to come back soon. She did not know how she had been able to hug her but she wanted to do so just once more.

Mable sat at her kitchen table cradling a cup of tea in her hands. She had been wandering around, unable to settle, since she had returned home and had now forced herself to sit down. The kitchen was warm from the heat of the AGA. Winter was almost here and the short days were getting colder. She stared into her mug. She had placed the centre tile that Flora had brought on the table together with the small brass key. She suddenly felt a prickling fear. What if the answers she was so desperate for were not inside the last journal? Or if Harriet was mistaken and the journal wasn't in the secret drawer at all.

She felt old. Though her face made her look like a young fifty, inside she felt the weight of every one of her one hundred and ninety-two years. Mable thought back to her conversation with Flora. Would she really take a cure if there was one? And what would happen to her if she did?

She thought about Flora and Archie. They were such good children. Archie had endured a lot. He almost seemed as if he had lived the same amount of years as she had. Mable felt like she understood him; she had learned a lot about people in her time. She liked Flora very much too. She was strong; a go-getter who would do well, despite the sadness she carried from not knowing her mother. Perhaps if she had them in her life, she would not feel so lonely.

Her mind drifted to Harriet, her friend. It had been

bittersweet to see her – a ghost who was still the girl that she would always remember. It had reminded her of the reality of her age and it had made her think of Joe.

Now it seemed that they would both get what they wanted. Mable would have her answers and Harriet would get her freedom. Perhaps it would free them both.

Flora gazed out of the classroom window. She liked maths, solving puzzles, creating patterns and learning formulae but her heart wasn't in it today.

Under the cover of the trees, the grass not yet touched by the sun, was dusty with frost. An awful lot had happened as the weeks had passed and the seasons had changed from autumn into winter. Her dream of being a detective had finally become real in a strange and surreal way. She could never have imagined it – a ghost and a one hundred and ninety-two year old lady – but if her Sherlock Holmes stories had taught her anything, it was that when you're solving a mystery, you often find the unexpected along the way.

She thought about Mable. She had come to like her a lot and she hoped that she would find the answers that she'd been waiting for. And Flora would never have believed in a trillion years that her dad's warehouse would be home to a ghost like Harriet. But when she thought about it, why shouldn't it be? The furniture and antiques had once been a part of somebody's life, why wouldn't they be connected in some way. Perhaps there were other ghosts who needed help.

A jolt of excitement charged through her when she thought of that, she would speak to Archie about it later.

Archie was drifting away from his English lesson. A book in his hand, the words were blurred and jumbling together. He had read the same sentence twelve times.

He was thinking about Mable. Nearly two hundred years old! He had always thought of living forever as an amazing power, but in reality, it had left Mable sad and alone. Archie felt a connection to Mable. She had no one to care for her, just like him if he hadn't had Flora.

He hoped that Mable would stay around so he could get to know her. He wanted to hear stories about her life. He wondered what it had been like to live on the frontiers of Canada. Archie decided that if she got her answers from the journal and she stayed, he would like to spend more time with her and let her know that she didn't need to be unhappy or lonely; he would be a friend to her like Flora was to him.

He smiled. Imagine! He'd been talking to a ghost! A few weeks ago he'd been more than freaked out when he'd been haunted, but now that the girl had spoken to him, well, he was still freaked out but perhaps not quite so much.

They were a good team, him and Flora. She was definitely Sherlock and although he wasn't quite so sure that he was Dr Watson, he had still managed to help her.

As long as there were no more ghosts! The thought of there being some in the warehouse made his knees shake. If he didn't see another ghost again, once they'd seen

Harriet one last time as they'd promised, then he would be very happy.

He read the same sentence for the thirteenth time and waited for the bell to ring.

CHAPTER THIRTY-FIVE

The doors creaked open as they had always done. The familiar, warm smell of spices and mothballs took her back to another life as she half-clambered inside. She wondered if she would fall through into Narnia; she'd always been superstitious about it.

Her fingers patted around the floor until she found it in the furthest left-hand corner – a small indentation with a tiny hole. Mable had to jiggle the key to get it to fit. She turned it with her fingertips and a gentle click announced that the compartment had opened. For a brief moment she thought of Joe, how clever he had been to make something so special. She reached inside a shoe-box sized recess and found what she was hoping for, then she backed out of the wardrobe as Archie and Flora held the doors open for her.

My experiments have turned out to be even more interesting than I could have imagined.

I collected two poor, begotten animals from the pound, saving them just before they were to be put out of their misery – and what terrible misery it was. A cat and a dog that had a catalogue of terrible ailments. The cat was suffering from a disease that had caused most of its fur to fall out; leaving only puss-filled, scabby skin that was severely infected. It had been hit by a carriage and from the blood around its nose and mouth was obviously suffering from internal injuries as well as a broken right leg. The dog had a broken front leg and was in such pain that it cried each time it took a step. It had been severely beaten and the skin across its back was raw with infection. Both animals were terribly malnourished and their ribs protruded like the edges of sharp knives. They were so close to death that they seemed completely unaware of one another. It was all I could do not to do the deed and put them down myself. The man at the pound thought I was quite mad as I carried them into my carriage.

Preparation:
I ground the seeds together with some water and made a poultice. I administered this poultice externally to the creatures' injuries, wrapping them in bandages so they would not nibble or chew. I left them overnight.

The following morning the cat was at death's door. I was more than surprised to see it hadn't died in the night and so named it Lucky. Its internal injuries were obviously devastating.

Day three:

For three days nothing has changed, the cat has hovered between life and death and the dog has whimpered in pain. I think it is only the food and milk that I have fed them that is keeping them alive.

Day four:

Something has occurred. The dog's injured leg appears to be less painful. When I examined it the dog did not wince and it walked tentatively on its foot without crying out. The sores on its back have changed too. The swelling has lessened and the raw skin appears to be a healthier colour. The cat's skin is also less putrefied and infected. I have decided to administer the seeds orally to Lucky, crushing them into some warm milk.

Day six:

I have continued to apply the poultice externally to both cat and dog and over the past two days their skin has begun to heal.

Day seven:

For seven days I have applied the poultice to the broken bones, raw and infected skin of both animals. I have also given Lucky a dose of seeds in warm milk each day but because she sleeps so much I am still unaware of the effect the ingested seeds are having on her. Each morning I expect to find her dead.

Day eight:

Something extraordinary has happened. This morning I awoke and went to check on the animals. During the night a transformation had taken place. The dog's paw was so completely healed that as soon as I let it from its cage it bounced around the laboratory in its pleasure to see me. Its fur has even begun to grow back.

When I let Lucky from her cage she leapt from it and onto my stool with the agility of a young cat. Her mangy fur, though not grown completely had the soft look and touch of a new kitten. Her injuries were gone. I sat on my stool and watched as both animals then went about the business of eating their breakfasts. I was stunned to the point of being unable to speak. My question is: If my seeds can cure a dog of its injuries and save a cat on the brink of death in such a short time period, then what could it do for a human?

These seeds are very precious. They have the capacity to cure not just external wounds and broken bones but deep and life-threatening internal injuries. If I could develop them into a medicinal drink, then who knows what I could do? But I have only one small glass pot remaining. I have used most of them on the animals, and whilst I have planted a few of the seeds in the small garden at the rear of my laboratory, none have developed.

My concerns are also growing. I have a deepening sense of unease; I believe that I am in danger, and now that these experiments have further provided me with evidence of the properties of these seeds I must stop writing and hide that which I have discovered. These are dangerous times and I fear that my enemies are getting closer.

I have one more notation to make before I take this journal and hide it. I have found someone to help me with a future experiment, a human donor who is willing to put themselves forward, someone who is very ill and whose life will soon end. Perhaps if I have the courage, I will write once again when these experiments have been conducted, but for now I will keep all future research in my mind – which I believe to be the safest place.

If I must, I will return to the Galapagos Archipelago and collect more seeds. The very nature of their origin and the immense, aged tortoises that they have sustained holds the key, I believe, to their miraculous life giving properties.

Sat in front of the fire in Mable's study, the three of them had been reading the journal between them for almost an hour, some of the words were difficult to decipher and although it was interesting, it was only the last couple of pages that held the information they really wanted.

'That's all there is,' Mable finally stated as she closed the book.

'Are you alright?' Flora asked, aware that Mable's mood had gone from excited to downcast and quiet.

'Yes I'm fine,' Mable said, 'It's just, I suppose I was expecting more. I was hoping for answers or at least for a conclusion and there isn't one.' She seemed crestfallen.

'But at least you do know some things that you didn't before,' said Archie. 'You know where the seeds came from and that those plants were eaten by the giant tortoises in the Galapagos Islands, which might explain a lot. Those tortoises live to well over a hundred years. You have somewhere to start. Then there's the bit about another subject, someone who was going to be the human guinea pig. Imagine if there was somebody just like you.'

'I know, I know,' Mable conceded. 'I was just expecting... more.'

'Such as?' Flora asked.

'Such as... a cure, a reason, an explanation as to why I've lived so long, why I am aging so very slowly. I don't know. But you're right, Archie, at least I know what plant the seeds came from. Perhaps we can have a look later on the Internet.'

'I *do* know what you mean, Mable. This journal seems

to be the beginning of his research; Charles Darwin wouldn't have known about the seeds causing such a long life, at least not unless he took them himself. What about Harriet's diary? There might be more clues in there,' Flora was curious to see what a young girl at the beginning of the Victorian age would have written about.

'I don't think so. She read Mr Darwin's other journals but wouldn't have had any time to write about them. The fire was that same night and I'm not sure we should read it,' Mable said, 'I think we should let Harriet decide that.'

'Yes, you're right,' Flora said understanding what Mable meant and feeling a little guilty. She would hate anyone to read her diary without her say so. 'We'll see her this evening. I'll have to go home first and take dad's spare keys, if we go soon he won't be there and he'll think we're still here. I have to say, though; I'm feeling really guilty about my dad. I would like to at least tell him something,' said Flora.

'Of course you must tell him something but perhaps not *everything*, and not just yet,' Mable smiled; she had brightened up a little, which made Flora feel better too.

'Why don't I make us something to eat and we'll leave after that,' Mable said.

They were quiet on the way back to Flora's house, each of them thinking about Charles Darwin's secret research.

Mable was wondering if Mr Darwin had ever gone back to the Galapagos and retrieved more of the 'miracle' seeds. They would surely have heard about it if he had. And why would he have passed on an opportunity to change the world? He obviously didn't know the full potential of those seeds, but he was certainly aware of their healing nature. What had happened to make him stay quiet about his incredible discovery? Though perhaps after the tragedy of the fire at March Lane he didn't have the heart to pursue it.

She wished that there had been more information about the seeds, specifically which plant they had come from. She felt like she was clutching at straws and there were no more answers to her questions.

Flora was worried about Mable. A cloud had settled over her and far from making her feel better, the journal had only seemed to make her sadder. But they did have one answer: they knew where the seeds had come from, that they'd come from a plant that the giant tortoises ate and, even though they might eat more than one type of plant, they could probably narrow it down. That would be an easy investigation.

She understood why Mable felt so low. She would have felt the same; there were no definite answers in the journal, like just *how long* Mable would continue to live? She knew that was what Mable had been hoping for. Flora could identify with that. Her mother had left her with an encyclopaedia of questions that would never be answered.

Archie was considering what he'd read. The seeds could hold the key to everything. He had a feeling though that it wasn't as simple as he'd first imagined. In those final pages, Charles Darwin had written about a human guinea pig – what if there was another person as old as Mable somewhere in the world?

He also wondered about Darwin's secrecy. Archie could understand keeping quiet about things at first, after all Darwin had waited almost twenty years to publish his book *On the Origin of Species*. But this other research was so incredible – why hadn't they ever heard of it?

Archie sympathised with Mable, it seemed to him that there were still too many questions and not enough answers.

It was difficult being a detective he finally concluded. Closing the door on one mystery only seemed to immediately open up another one.

CHAPTER THIRTY-SIX

The warehouse was freezing as they climbed the stairs to the third floor yet again. Colin was in his kennel, this time he'd refused to come out even when they'd called him.

Flora had phoned her dad and told him they would be another hour. He was happy to know that she was with Archie and Mable, but Flora was glad that she would finally be able to explain things to him once the evening was over.

It seemed like years since they had found the sooty floor tiles, and even though she was anxious, Flora felt a thrill at the thought of seeing Harriet again. This time she would try to speak to her without her voice giving away how scared she was.

Flora carefully held the two journals as they entered the tile room.

'Harriet, are you there?' Mable called out.

The apprehension was visible on Archie's face as he stepped closer to Flora, their arms touching. She smiled, trying to reassure him.

It was much colder in the room this time. Their breath came out in misty plumes and then as the light bulb began to flicker Harriet appeared.

'Hello, my friends,' she said brightly.

Mable jumped. Harriet's voice boomed inside their heads.

'You startled me!' Mable said then suddenly laughed.

'It is wonderful to see you again,' Harriet said, 'and I know that you have the journal and my diary – at last! I felt it.' Flora held both books out towards her.

'Thank you, Flora but I cannot take them. I just wanted to be sure that my dear friend Lily had them.'

Flora cleared her throat, 'Um, we read Charles Darwin's journal but we didn't read your diary. What would you like us to do with it?'

'Oh that's thoughtful of you, but you may read it if you wish. I will not be embarrassed. I'm sure you will find that the writings are the same as any girl of our age, despite our very different eras of time,' Harriet said wistfully. 'More importantly,' she turned to Mable, 'did you find the answers to your questions?'

Mable's face changed, 'A little but not as much as I would have liked.'

'Oh no!' Harriet exclaimed, her dismay was clear, 'But that is the very reason I am here! I am certain of it. I was to help you find the journal so that you would have the solutions that you longed for.' She sounded so upset that Flora moved towards her, wanting to comfort her.

'I'm sure it is, and I *have* learned something. I know where the seeds came from and, with a little research and some travelling perhaps, I can discover more. The journal has given me a place to begin,' Mable said trying to reassure Harriet.

'Really? Then that is an answer, if only a small one. Where did they come from? I did not read the last journal, don't forget, and even though I lived with it here every day I was never able to take it from the wardrobe,' said Harriet.

'Mr Darwin wrote that the seeds came from the Galapagos Islands, from the plant that the giant tortoises ate,' Mable replied.

'Oh my!' Harriet exclaimed and then she slumped down on the floor.

Mable, Flora and Archie went quickly to her.

'Whatever is the matter, Harriet?' asked Mable, concerned.

Harriet smiled at them.

'That is the only answer you really need!' she laughed.

Mable shook her head, 'I don't understand.'

'The seeds that I gave to you on the night of the fire are the very same seeds that I grew in the glass house when Papa brought them back from his travels.'

'You mean they were from the Galapagos Islands too?' Mable asked.

Harriet jumped up and took Mable's hand. 'Yes. Don't you remember me telling you?'

'No I don't. I hated gardening then. I remember how foolish I thought you were, excited about planting some little seeds, but I don't recall you telling me where they came from.'

'Papa collected them but he couldn't have told Mr Darwin that my seeds had thrived. I think that Mr Darwin had been too distracted with all that he was doing. He obviously didn't know that I had managed to grow the plants in our garden, or perhaps he didn't know that they had both collected the same seeds.'

'Mr Darwin wrote that he was running out of the seeds and that he might have to return to the Galapagos to get more. He couldn't have known,' said Archie, beginning to understand what Harriet and Mable were talking about.

'Then don't you see? That is why I am here, so that I could tell you that the very seeds that have given you this long life are growing in *your* garden at March Lane!' Harriet jumped up and began to skip around the room, her feet not touching the dusty floorboards.

'You mean the star grasses are the same plant!?' exclaimed Mable.

'Yes, yes, yes,' Harriet continued to skip.

'I... I didn't even think. Joe told me that he had helped you to grow the plants, and that they had come from a hot country. Why didn't *he* know they were from the Galapagos Islands?'

'He knew that the seeds he helped me to plant had come from Papa's travels, but when I gave them to you on the night of the fire I just took the pot from the sack. I didn't tell him what they were. You said yourself he didn't see *what* I had tipped into your mouth. How would he ever have guessed without reading the journals? Even if he had known the seeds' origin, you still wouldn't have made the connection until you'd read Mr Darwin's journal.

'Remember, I was told you were dying and then Papa and I left without speaking to either of you again. I was too sad to talk to anyone,' Harriet stopped skipping, she frowned, 'But you still don't know why or how the seeds worked.'

'But that doesn't matter, don't you see?' said Mable her excitement building. 'The grasses are still growing in the garden at March Lane. They've flowered every year that I have lived there and they reminded me of you and Joe so much. We now have the source of the seeds! Somehow, I will find out everything about them and the plants they come from. I will be able to carry out my own experiments and perhaps *I* will be able to find a cure!'

'Of course! I was right. The journal was the key to the whole story – to *your* story, Lily!' Harriet skipped around the room again then she suddenly stopped. She spoke very quietly. 'I think it is time.' She was looking above them towards the skylight.

The light bulb began to flicker and in a blink she was next to Flora and Archie. She reached forward and drew Flora into a hug. Flora gasped as she felt a calming warmth flow through her.

'Thank you, Flora, you are the best detective, don't ever stop helping others,' Harriet said gently to her.

Then she stepped towards Archie. Archie braced himself, but when Harriet held him he felt a strange lightness flutter inside his chest. 'I wish we could have been friends,' Harriet whispered. Archie surprised himself by suddenly wishing the same thing.

Harriet turned to Mable, who was crying. She went to her and hugged her.

'Please don't cry, dear Lily, be happy for me. Papa is there,' Harriet looked at the skylight again, 'Oh! And Mama too! She is waving, calling me...' Harriet's voice was filled with happiness.

Even though she could see nothing through the skylight, Mable said softly to her friend, 'They are waiting for you. I think you can leave now. Go to them.'

Mable took Harriet's hand and walked with her to a place just underneath the skylight. Outside, the dark sky sparkled with stars.

Harriet smiled at them and said, 'Goodbye my dear, Lily. Goodbye Flora and Archie, I have left you all something as a thank you.'

And then she was gone.

On the dusty floor beneath the skylight lay the drawing of Harriet with her mama and papa outside March Lane.

CHAPTER THIRTY-SEVEN

At home again, Flora and Archie lay on the carpet in Flora's bedroom. They had been still and quiet for almost an hour.

Mable had left them at the warehouse gates with an excited promise to see them both soon.

Flora had been thinking about their meeting with Harriet. She couldn't forget the feeling of when Harriet hugged her. It was as though all of her worries had gone, like she was so carefree and light that at any moment she could have lifted herself from the floor and floated around her room. She laughed out loud and Archie smiled.

'Sounds like you're feeling the same as me,' he said, hardly able to understand the joy that he felt.

'I know! Can you believe it? It's as if there is no problem that can't be solved and nothing that will ever worry me again,' Harriet grinned at him.

'You're right! Like nothing is impossible! All the stuff with my mum doesn't matter anymore because I feel so happy, so content, that it can't faze me ever again. Does that make sense?'

'Yes,' said Flora.

'I wonder how she did it?' said Archie thoughtfully.

'Do you think that Mable felt the same? I mean, Harriet

touched her too. Perhaps this is what it always feels like when you're touched by a ghost.'

'Well as nice at it is I'm not planning on touching any more.'

Flora laughed.

'No really, Flora. I mean it...'

'You can't possibly mean it! You heard what Harriet said, there are loads of other ghosts in the warehouse, and if we helped her then perhaps we can help another. We could be the ghost detectives! Our speciality: solving all problems of a ghostly nature.'

'You know that amazing feeling I was talking about? Well it's just disappeared. Are you serious?'

'Of course I'm serious. We solved a mystery for a ghost and a one hundred and ninety-two year old lady. It wasn't exactly a crime but we did it just the same. Perhaps we could help someone else.' Flora took Archie's hand, 'We make an amazing team, Archie.'

Archie looked down at Flora's hand holding his, 'I suppose we do.'

'Will you think about it?'

'Alright,' said Archie.

'Although I'm not sure how we would communicate with the ghosts that are in the warehouse. We've been playing there for years and Harriet was the first contact we've ever had,' said Flora. Flora squeezed Archie's hand. 'But don't worry Archie. I'll do the talking.'

She knew that he would need some persuading but she also knew he would be beside her no matter what. They were best friends.

The mood came back in a wave again and she closed her eyes and enjoyed it while it lasted.

Mable watched the fire as she sipped her tea. Despite the freezing night the room was warm, and she could feel the heat from the fire on her legs. She felt happy, happier than she'd felt in almost a hundred and forty years – since Joe had died. She was sure it was because Harriet had hugged her. All her concerns, and her deep sadness had melted, as if Harriet had taken them with her to wherever she had gone.

Finally, she had answers. She now knew why she had lived so long, and that very reason was growing in her garden. She would harvest the next batch of seeds from Harriet's star grasses and make a start on trying to decipher how and why they worked. She had money and time, plenty of time, to make and complete all the necessary plans and experiments, even if it took her another hundred years, she now had a real purpose.

She also had friends, Flora and Archie, and even Horace. The first people she could call friends in a long, long time. She was sure that Horace would be as understanding and as discreet as Flora when they finally told him the truth. Perhaps that was another reason she felt happy. The loneliness she had felt for so long had gone.

Mable got up from the armchair and put the guard in front of the fire. The flames were dying and it would soon be out. She closed the door to the study and walked along the hallway towards the kitchen. She stopped for a moment, still hardly able to believe what she was seeing. The tile floor that had always belonged in the house at March Lane was returned and in its rightful place. The floor that she had spent much of her early life cleaning and polishing, sparkled like she had been down on her knees scrubbing it not an hour before, but of course she hadn't.

This was Harriet's gift to her.

Even the centre tile was in place. She could not even begin to understand how it had happened, but then she was almost two hundred years old and she knew that there were many things that could never be explained.

The floor and her happiness were both restored.

Mable reached the kitchen. An old tea chest that she'd fetched from the attic to keep the journal, Harriet's diary and the little brass key safe in, was on the table. The Mathias family portrait lay next to it, the drawing which had appeared under the skylight in the warehouse, just as it had dropped from the album.

Mable decided that she would give the diary to Flora when she saw her next. She had been party to most of the secrets inside it anyway, and she knew that Flora would appreciate it.

She went to the sink to swill out her cup. As she glanced out of the window she saw something move in the garden. She stepped back. There was a pale half-moon in the sky. Without hesitating she reached for her coat which was hung on the back of the door. She turned the key and stepped outside. A hard, cold wind caught her breath as she stood on the patio. Waiting for her eyes to adjust to the weak moonlight she walked slowly towards the greenhouse as she realised what she had seen.

The grass, which was almost as tall as she was, had begun to flower. Harriet's stars! All around her as far as she could see the winter blooms had blossomed. They stood high and proud, dancing with the wind. The smell of their honey perfume overwhelmed her. She put out her hands and brushed her fingertips over the star shaped heads; then she threw back her head and laughed.

CHAPTER THIRTY-EIGHT

Flora dragged herself out of bed. It was Saturday morning and she'd promised to help her dad. Archie had slept over in the spare room and her dad had woken them early for breakfast.

Last night they had agreed to tell her father everything over their fish and chip supper later. Flora felt certain that he would take everything that they had to tell him in his stride, as he did with everything else in his life. In fact, she and Archie couldn't really remember why they hadn't told him sooner.

They both felt light-headed as they jumped in the van. The contented feeling remained. It had faded a little, though not in a bad way. Flora thought it felt a bit like Boxing Day, when the excitement of Christmas is over but there are still presents and the school holidays to enjoy!

Colin greeted Flora as he normally did by ignoring her dad and Archie, and almost knocking her over with his enthusiasm; he was his old self again. She gave him a treat from her pocket and smoothed his soft ears.

'Back to normal now boy,' she said quietly to him.

And that was when it happened.

A gentle whisper that could almost have been missed. *Almost.*

Archie's face told her that he'd heard it too. Colin's ears flattened and he bounded off in the direction of his kennel.

She heard a voice, and then another, and then another. There were lots of voices saying her name, Archie's too and they were all trying to speak to them at the same time. Archie was very flustered.

Her dad had already unlocked the warehouse and was calling them to get out of the cold as he disappeared inside.

'I have a feeling that this is the thank you gift that Harriet said she was giving us,' Flora said to Archie.

'I thought it was the Mathias family drawing appearing out of nowhere, but I think you're right. We said we didn't hear any other ghosts and now we can hear flipping hundreds of them. We're going to be dead busy trying to solve mysteries for all of them' said Archie tensely.

Flora started to giggle.

'What?' asked Archie, he didn't sound happy.

'You said "dead" busy,' Flora laughed.

'Oh no!' said Archie as he grinned and began to laugh too.

In the highest, darkest place of the warehouse a man waited. His colours were indistinct, as if he had just stepped from a sepia photograph. A deep scar dragged the corner of his right eye downwards and distorted his face. He was restless and knew that he was trapped, he could not escape. He needed help to leave and he would do anything to get that help. Anything at all...

Available from Candy Jar Books

SILENT MOUNTAIN

by Michelle Briscombe

Jack Jupiter is not cool, he is not brave and he is altogether unremarkable. With constant bullying at school, Jack buries himself in a wildlife book given to him by his father.

When his gran predicts that 'the freeze' is going to happen, Jack cannot resist the urge to test her prophecy.

At the frozen lake he finds much more than he expected. He is drawn into a thrilling and dangerous adventure, where fantastical creatures and unrelenting enemies lead Jack to discover the truth about his father and the mythical Silent Mountain.

ISBN: 978-0-9571548-1-0

Also available from Candy Jar Books

AMULET
by Alison Thomas

A magical story of cave dwellers, clowns and vegetarian dragons.

Dion has Asperger's Syndrome. He is an intelligent boy who lives in the functional ordered world.

When he is kidnapped and taken to a place beyond the imagination, Dion finds that his disciplined mind becomes strength. But little does he realise his life is now in danger.

Will his sister Megan get to him in time? Not if the evil Queen has anything to do with it.

For a boy who doesn't like change. Dion's strength and determination is the one thing he will have to rely on.

ISBN: 978-0-9933221-6-7

Also available from Candy Jar Books

THINNER THAN WATER

by Sue Hampton

Kim Braddock and Fizzy Duvall have never met. Kim's a passionate footballer with a repertoire of impressions, a temper and a dark sense of humour. Fizzy's a shy, romantic idealist who wants to please everyone.

All they have in common is a very big city, one black parent and one white – and the same fifteenth birthday.

When their identities are overturned, they form a bond that changes them both as two families struggle with the truth. But as conflict deepens, is their connection strong enough to survive?

Fiction for young adults aged 13+

"Thinner Than Water is an enjoyable and fascinating read. This is a fantastic template for an onscreen drama."
Beverley Knight

ISBN: 978-0-9931191-0-1

TOMMY PARKER: Destiny Will Find You

by Anthony Ormond

When Tommy Parker packs his bag and goes to his grandpa's house for the summer he has no idea that his life is about to change forever.

But that's exactly what happens when his grandpa lets him in on a fantastic secret. He has a pen that lets him travel through his own memories and alter the past. Imagine that! Being able to travel into your own past and re-write your future.

Tommy Parker: Destiny Will Find You! is an exhilarating adventure that redefines the time travel genre.

You'll never look at your memories in quite the same way again...

ISBN: 978-0-9928607-1-4

Also available from Candy Jar Books

DOCTOR WHO EDITION

Space, Time, Machine, Monster: Doctor Who Edition takes you on a journey into the science of *Doctor Who.*

Jam-packed with aliens, time machines, spaceships and lots of monsters, this book explores the secrets of the Universe's favourite Time Lord.

And, for an extra bit of fun, we present our own *Doctor Who* Top 10s on topics such as planets, companions, favourite stories and catchphrases!

So how does a Dalek poo? Let's find out!

ISBN: 978-0-9933221-3-6

Also available from Candy Jar Books

LETHBRIDGE-STEWART: THE FORGOTTEN SON
by Andy Frankham-Allen

For Colonel Alistair Lethbridge-Stewart his life in the Scots Guards was straightforward enough; rising in the ranks through nineteen years of military service. But then his regiment was assigned to help combat the Yeti incursion in London, the robotic soldiers of an alien entity known as the Great Intelligence. For Lethbridge-Stewart, life would never be the same again.

Meanwhile in the small Cornish village of Bledoe a man is haunted by the memory of an accident thirty years old. The Hollow Man of Remington Manor seems to have woken once more. And in Coleshill, Buckinghamshire, Mary Gore is plagued by the voice of a small boy, calling her home.

What connects these strange events to the recent Yeti incursion, and just what has it all to do with Lethbridge-Stewart?

"A solid start to the series. The Brigadier is such an integral part of Doctor Who mythos, it seems right and proper he now has his own series." – Doctor Who Magazine

ISBN: 978-0-9931191-5-6